ADVANCE PRAISE FOR

"D. Foy's writing is so rich, so
literature, that one is tempted to st
whatever madcap equivalencies ("It's X meets Y!") might begin to describe it accurately. Yet its whorl and grain, the fantastical strangeness of Foy's sentences and the astonishing accuracy of his perception, amounts to something I can only call new. *Made to Break* is that rare thing: a truly original, and ferociously necessary, book."
—MATTHEW SPECKTOR

"*Made to Break* is a fearless exploration of fragility—the fragility of friendship, the fragility of romance, the fragility of human life—but the book itself, trussed by D. Foy's lavishly constructed sentences and astute psychological observations, is built to last. Think: Céline. Think: Burroughs. Think: Denis Johnson. Or better yet, think: D. Foy, poet laureate-elect of that marginal America filled with junkies and drunks, where death is omnipresent, and the refuge of an open diner on a stormy night is the closest one gets to the American Dream."
—ADAM WILSON

"While reading *Made to Break* I just couldn't believe it was the author's first novel. The characters are deadly, troubled, vibrant, and their world is suffused with evil—not the manufactured evil of a Hollywood horror movie, but the carefully paced malevolence of a world doomed to swallow its inhabitants, consuming their shallow, fucked up memories in a swell of amoral darkness. D. Foy is not just a writer. He's the kind of archangel Stanley Kubrick would have built wings for. Don't just read this book. Revel in it. I swear you won't be able to stop."
—SAMUEL SATTIN

# MADE TO BREAK

A NOVEL BY

D. FOY

TWO DOLLAR RADIO
*Books too loud to ignore.*

**TWO DOLLAR RADIO** is a family-run outfit founded in 2005 with the mission to reaffirm the cultural and artistic spirit of the publishing industry.

We aim to do this by presenting bold works of literary merit, each book, individually and collectively, providing a sonic progression that we believe to be too loud to ignore.


ISBN: 978-1-937512-16-3
Library of Congress Control Number: 2014930484

**Author photograph:** Snorri Sturluson
**Cover photographs:** (background) David Falconer, Photographer/Environmental Protection Agency, 1973; (overlay) NASA/CXC/CfA/S.Wolk et al.

You can see a short interview with D. Foy here: **https://vimeo.com/70723153**

Typeset in Garamond, the best font ever.
Printed in the United States of America.

TWO DOLLAR RADIO
*Books too loud to ignore.*
www.TwoDollarRadio.com
twodollar@TwoDollarRadio.com

For Jeanine

In no sense sober, we barbershopped together and never heard the discords in our music or saw ourselves as dirty, cheap, or silly.

— William H. Gass

# MADE
# TO
# BREAK

*I never said,* This is nothing more than words on water, *but something inside me knew it the same, like the world won't count what isn't there. I saw everything, but nothing made me see. I heard everything, but nothing made me hear. I knew nothing of how things begin or end, I was just an animal. Then I walked through a door in the hand of a woman who knew I'd fallen but didn't care. In so many words she'd said,* I'm with you today—isn't that what matters? *There in the midst of laughter and warmth, an unveiling had begun. All I'd known in the days before was a lie. I myself was a liar and a lie…*

CHRISTMAS EVE WORD GOT OUT LUCILLE HAD been taken by the real world, of corporate jobs and big-big coin. Christmas Day the scene was on. As for that affair, the only thing I know for sure is some time close to three or four we laid into a mound of dope. But now the New Year was two days off, and what had been a mound of dope was just a dirty mirror…

Locked into four-by at eighty-plus, we were headed for Tahoe, and Dinky's family cabin. The radio was playing some power-pop group, Ring Finger, I think it was.

*I gave it all up for you,*
*and I'm happy today,*
*yeah my sky is blue today!*

*It's true little baby,*
*we're a thing called us,*
*all shiny and new—*
*the brand new me*
*and super new you!*

Of course by the time we hit Bridal Veil Falls, the tank was dry, and we were stuck. Hickory nudged me as she pointed to the sign.

"Romantic," I said.

"Nice," Dinky said.

And then we were trekking through rain, to some joint up the road he thought had fuel. An hour and a half got us four blistered feet and a defunct inn that looked like a Swiss chalet. When finally a man brought us gas, we headed down the mountain for more. A pack of tourists had crowded the inn the second time round, waiting for some guy to fix their flat. Basil dropped drawer and stuck his ass to the window while Lucille assaulted the horn. "Idiots!" we shouted…

Truth was the cabin in lights through a swirl of ice and rain. We'd nothing to do but get to the door, but the stairs slipped me up, and I collapsed, and lost my bottle, too… The stars were dead. The night was rage. The earth was sick with danger. Someone moaned, and from the blue I understood: time is a leech… And then a butcher jumped my head, a squat little man with an Abe Lincoln beard and collection of filthy knives. And then when I heard the breaking glass, the butcher turned and vanished…

Basil had smashed a window with his hatchet after Dinky confessed he'd lost his key. Now the giant appeared at the door with an arm swept out in phony cheer. I remembered once a girl called him handsome.

"*Entrez-vous*," he said.

"You smell that?" I said about the stink.

"Whoo-wee!" said Lucille.

"I smoke," Basil said. "I can't smell dick."

"I can assure you," Hickory said. "This is not the smell of dick."

We headed to the kitchen for glasses and ice, the scent growing stronger, a compound more like mildew and vanilla.

"Oh goody," Basil said.

There was nothing in the fridge but the little bags of glop people use for wounds.

My hand knocked Basil's hat to the floor, the porkpie his grandfather gave him a decade back. The doof had been wearing it all this time, every day but Christmas.

"If it's not one thing," I said, "it's your mother."

Dinky flipped the light. "Christ on a crutch," he said.

On the floor, in a bamboo cage with pits and dung, lay a lovebird dead as wood.

"Now *that*," Basil said, tapping the cage with his boot, "is some weird-ass shit."

Hickory looked at Dinky. "You're not going to tell me this was yours, I hope."

"We've never seen the thing."

"Maybe," I said, "it was your grandpa's."

"Granddad hates animals. He wouldn't let Dad have a fish."

Lucille had been picking at her lip so long her mouth looked like a steak. "I had a bird once," she said. "When we lived in Carolina."

"That's very nice, Lucille," Dinky said. "Thank you for sharing that with us."

She ignored this and shuffled closer. "It was a finch. Then one day I came home from school, and she was gone."

"It flew away?" Hickory said.

"Her name was Zoë," Lucille said, and put a hand to her face. The stink was really nuts. "My father said if he had to hear that racket for one more day, he'd be forced to use his gun."

"You ever hear a finch?" I said. "Not loud at all. Finches are about the nicest bird around."

"He hated cleaning its cage, is what I think."

I left the kitchen as Hickory told Basil to dump the bird. He complained at first, but then a door slammed and slammed again, and there they were, Dinky and Basil, huffing at their smokes.

Lucille had laid out a dog-eared copy of *Fear and Loathing* next to a stack of discs. She jabbed the On button, then Play—out came "Bela Lugosi's Dead."

"So who's going to get the ice?"

I told her she had two legs.

"Excuse me?"

She was always making people repeat themselves. It gave her notions of power.

"Turn that down," I said. She waited a second before turning it down. "I said you've got two legs."

"You ought to know. You've been staring at them long enough."

"Check the TV," Dinky said. "We want to see if they're still saying it's going to flood."

"It's the day before New Year's Eve," Basil said, as if the weather played to dates.

Dinky ran through the channels till he reached a woman with hair like GI Joe's. On the screen beside her flashed bombed-out streets and men at guns, perched on inexorable tanks. Another face appeared, a weeping crone, trailed by a man with a shapka and fatigues. The anchorwoman sat with considered reserve. Her voice was a tool for faith. *Operation Joint Endeavor*, she said, *appears to have reached a point of…*

Dinky squealed like he'd won a prize. "That's Atherton," he said. "From *our* company!" He knelt by the tube and gestured toward some pimply kid in a truck. "Jesus, that's our whole frigging company!"

"So much for your fifteen minutes, huh, Dink?" I said.

"You know I can't drink my whiskey without ice," Lucille said.

"Snow's good," Basil said. "Use snow."

"We're going to draw straws," Lucille said. "The two with the shortest get to make a run."

Dinky shook a bottle. "But we don't need no ice. We need *bourbon*. And as we can all see, we have *mas* bourbon."

"*No mas* no more, *pinche*," Lucille said, and squeezed Dinky's ass.

We cut the straw from a broom in the kitchen. Then Basil took the longest, Hickory the next, Lucille after that.

"Welly, welly, welly, welly, welly, welly, well," Basil said.

"Sorry," Hickory said.

Dinky looked like he might cry. "Why's it always me that's getting the shaft?"

"Cause you're feeble," Lucille said. "And jinxed."

"*Hatchet Lady*," Basil said, classic. "So mean."

"Just remember whose cabin you're in," Dinky said. "We're here for a week."

I punched Basil's arm. "Hey, asshole. You get rid of the bird?"

THE ROAD WAS RUNNY AND BLACK, AND WHEN the lights hit the trees they looked like creeping skin. A DJ yammered about our noses and what Jack Frost had done.

"So whose idea was it," Dinky said. But instead of taking his bait, like usual, I waited. He said, "We know you're familiar with the word *moronic*, Andrew. We won't talk about how we spent the last nine months in a place so cold your pee breaks on the ground. We'll save that for our golden years. You know what we need?"

I stared at him. He didn't want an answer. He'd ask you a goddamned question just to answer himself.

"What we need," he said, "is *Hawaii*. What we need is *Guam*. Girls in grass skirts and pigs with apples in their traps. Mai tais is what we need, AJ." And the gloopy bastard never drove with his hands at ten and two, either. One of them flapped about as he talked while the other hung across the wheel like an old rubber chicken. "How," he said, "are we ever supposed to get Hickory on her back when all she can think about is misery?"

I fiddled with the radio. I pulled down the visor to hate my face in the mirror. "You take a look in the mirror these days?"

"You know we don't like mirrors."

"Look at you. Look at your head. *Especially* your head. You were planning to get laid with that thing?"

Dinky started coughing so bad he stopped in the road. "We did fine in Germany," he said. Then he saw my retard's face and hit the gas. "You know, with the chicks."

"The *chick*, you mean. I saw her picture. She looked like a fat albino parrot. Not to mention she's a professional thief. Not to mention she gave you the clap."

"Fortunately for us, Uncle Sam takes care of his boys."

I studied the water on the window as it turned to pearls and marveled at the creatures in their snowbound lairs. I thought about my grandmother, how she answered the phone to say she'd been raped, or lost her child, or found a bag of stones. She hobbled from my flat one day, and when I asked her purpose, she said, *Home.*

"This thing in four-by?" I said.

"What do we think?"

"We think we should get the lead out."

The road had just two lanes. Trees flashed by, now sparkling, now black, a strobic land of bugaboos dreamed and real. We saw no cars, no people, not even the twinkle of lights on another unnamed road. The Cruiser heaved with empty cans and cigarette butts, a single dirty sock. And roasted peanuts and peanut shells, Basil had tossed them everywhere, the dashboard, the seats, one was in my hair. It stunk of laundry hampers, and ragamuffin carnivals, sculleries from days of yore…

My old toad once brought me to a creek bottom full of sycamore and oak. Everything shone in hues of green, lancets of sun pushing through the shadows. An odor of struggle suffused the air. It was the odor of springtime, of birth. High overhead a worry of jays had attacked a nest of fledglings. When my toad climbed a stone to piss the creek, I made my way to the tree. Shells lay about, and in fact a fledgling too, blue as tainted meat and with its tiny quaking eyes utterly pathetic. I took stock.

Gone as God my old toad was, wandered off, not a soul could tell. I trusted in his return, however, if only to grill me, that much no doubt I'd learned. At my feet the fledgling sawed away with its little grey beak, gasping and sawing with a relentlessness only its mortality in the offing could afford. Christ but what I would've given to flee that place, what meager breath as witness to this struggle I myself could draw, the creature's eyes watching mine, or rather not watching mine, not watching anything likely. To think otherwise had been absurd. They were like drops of shuddering ink, those eyes, so tiny, goddamn it, so sad, so full of such terrible, newborn horror that to call them eyes at all was somehow blasphemous. And the eyes of birds have never been the same. *Answer me!* they seemed to say. *Answer!* But I had no answer. And anyhow, *I*? Not even the nobility of silence was sufficient to that demand. Nothing was sufficient. I poked at the creature with a twig, and then with my toe I flipped it over, and then with my heel I crushed it...

"The army say anything to you about that bark of yours?" I said.

"The army doesn't say anything unless you get your arm blown off."

"You could pay down the debt yourself, you know. If you'd just get serious."

"How much more serious can we get than clearing mines from a war zone in the middle of hellish winter?"

"Pass the bar, Dinky. Do the law."

"There's no need to torture us, you know."

"I'm all gold," I said, and took another slug. "If nothing else you got the name for it."

"Now, class," Dinky said with the nasally voice he assumed to mock himself. "Why is it we think Stuyvesant Wainwright the Fourth has failed the bar six times?" He raised his eyebrows and spoke in singsong cadence. "*Because he didn't learn anything in school but how to do lots and lots of drugs and drink lots and lots of booze*. Let that," he said, "be a lesson in how to fail."

"And get sick," I said.

For an instant through the trees the casinos glimmered down the strip. The dealers hung tight in those mad shops, I knew how, working the gamblers to their rings. Where was Hickory—her eyes, her mouth, the voice that purred from it?

"The army," said Dinky, raising his arm strongman-like. "*That* takes youth."

He turned at me to grin. Which is why I thought he might not've seen the mudslide on the road, though in truth he had, because all at once his eyes popped out, and we went lurching this way and that until we broke into a spin that closed on a bank of stones.

I woke up to a land of dark. Neither Dinky nor I said a word. We just sat there in the cold, and all that giant black seemed to've swallowed up the world. Where were all the lovely people? Where were all the vermin, and where were all the stars?

When finally I got the nerve to look at my friend, he was pinned in his seat by the wheel. It wasn't until I'd begun to think maybe he was knocked out, maybe even dead, that he wriggled free. Out in the night, he looked like one of those freaks you see on *Ripley's Believe It or Not!*, the one abducted by Martians. He stood there for a minute, then staggered off and fell in the mud.

"It used to be when I coughed I heard bees in my head. Now all I hear is fire."

"Write a poem about it sometime," I said, and scanned the road.

"AJ… AJ…" And then, "Please."

"We're buddies," I told him. "Remember?"

Mud rushed down the mountain. The rain was an opaque sheet. I held Dinky's head and waited.

"Get me that bourbon, would you?"

And then we heard an engine, a song for all we cared, followed by lights through the dark and, again, after something like an epoch, a truck round the bend.

"You see that, buddy?" I said, waving my arms. "That's your guardian angel. We'll be home in a minute."

BASIL HAD NO BALLS TO JUMP LUCILLE TILL THE stretch last summer at San Quintín. Dinky had passed out that night, though it wouldn't have mattered. Sooner or later she'd have left him as she did. Nearly five whole years they'd stuck it out—a goodish while in the buddy world, an eon or two for her. It was midnight on the beach, the moon was making hay. I'd stuffed my pockets with silver dollars and fireworks, and packets of musty Chiclets. The fine grey sand was dancing everywhere, across the dunes and slick opalescence where the water meets the shore. When at last I spied them in a hollow of grass, Lucille was bouncing like the bluest blue-movie girl the boys have ever seen. Doubtless neither had meant to hurt our friend. What were they, anyhow, but two sad dolts caught up in the malice of affairs? Lucille wasn't as mean back then, either, not like she'd come to be. She was free from the fear of her corporate future, if in fact that's what it had been. Nor did Basil ever hold ills, nothing genuine at least. He was a single child. He only knew to take what he saw. I never expected more. Still, they should've known better than to play with the clan. We'd pledged allegiance to it like a flag: *Buddies forever*, we'd promised, and we were solemn. But today things were different. I knew it. Dinky knew it, too. We all did. And now to prove it he was sprawled in a storm with his bottle, waiting for the guy that had just rolled up to save us.

First thing I noticed was the monkey—dead—dangling from the mirror on a string of beads. It could've been a fetus of hair, this thing, with pebbles for eyes and corn for teeth. The man that had hung it sat motionless behind the wheel, clad in weathered denim. He had sunken cheeks and hollow eyes and a silver beard to boot. I scratched my ear—his eyes traced my hand. I drummed my fingers—his eyes traced my hand. Klaus Kinski came to mind, as Herzog's Nosferatu, and grunions filled my head, beneath a heavy moon. We were alone.

"That little flake," said the man as he nodded to the monkey, "is called José." He sucked a tooth and gestured to a crucifix he himself must have painted red. "Ronald, though, he's not so bad as Fortinbras or him." Tattooed across the fingers of one hand was the word BEND, across the other, GIVE. A cigarette twitched in the webbing there. Empties fouled the dash.

"We hit a bear," I said.

Why I did I couldn't say. We'd had an accident. What difference how? Maybe I feared any less a case for invading the old man's turf—and sure as shit I had such a feeling, like I'd missed some glaring portent of doom, I didn't know—would send him on a rampage. Or maybe it was just his creepy gaze.

"Who's that?" he said. Dinky was still in the mud.

"He's sick."

"I see, I see, so that's who he is."

"Listen, mister, we need a ride bad."

"You need something bad," said the man. In slow order he tapped the Christ, the monkey, and the yellow dog beside him. "What do you fellows think R-E this crisis?" I stood waiting while he sucked his teeth some more and spit. "Throw him in," he said with a jerk of his thumb to the rear.

"He's *sick*," I said.

"You hear that, Fortinbras?" he said to the dog.

I found no change in the geeze's tone, but Fortinbras dropped from the window and appeared in the bed behind him. A spate of dolls in varied dismemberment lay about the beast, some missing heads, others arms or legs. The man shot me a look part fishy, part fatherly, his eyes running off two ways at once.

"You going to lay one, boy, or get off the pot?"

I wanted to be naked, to lie naked beneath a tender sun. I wanted the smell of a clean bright day, and heat, tart and dry. I wanted a heat that lasted, endless sand, visions of dazzle and grain. Why wouldn't his eyes release me?... *Lanterns, vultures, many things in hell... I made up my mind to take the life of the old man, and thus rid myself of the eye forever... Madmen know nothing...*

I got Dinky in the cab. The man took my hand. It was smooth and hard and cold as outer space.

"The name is Super."

"Andrew," I said. "That's Dinky."

"Pleased to rub truth with you boys."

"We could use a doctor now, I think."

Super gripped his wheel. "You do what you've done, you'll get what you've got. Catch our drift?"

Dinky drew himself up to look at this strange man. "We hate doctors," he said.

"Then which way you going?" I said.

"The only way that's good," Super said, "and that's the way we come."

"That *is* good," Dinky said with a smile. "Because we sure do hate a doctor."

BIRDFEED AND BULLETS, THE WEEPING BARK OF A million pines…

A freezer's scent of the clinic and the morgue…

The gleam of a roadside can…

The road wound on, the road kept winding, and sound was a cat's rough tongue…

Super's face was constant motion—that silver beard, those leathery cheeks, tiny eyes that flitted and bounced…

He ranted and sang and whispered and howled, and he did it all with ease…

We'd been forsaken, more or less, adrift with the phantoms that were the old man's words, loosed, it seemed, with each wave of his troubling hand…

At some point he set in about the doings in our cabin, inexplicable, he said, slippery, he said, though never exactly what…

I saw the lovebird, its gaping beak and eyes, I smelled ice cream and road kill and blood…

That familiar longing had returned, for my noons of summer, counting minnows in a jar and naming each breeze. What had happened to those days?

A meerschaum appeared in Super's hand and then from the glove a bag of gnarly weed, but Dinky went on drooling. Super crammed the stuff in the pipe and with a nail snicked the match he'd somehow managed to keep…

He chortled and smiled, puffed and drove, happy is as happy can…

I took the pipe, he the bottle…

The road was thick with water and mud and stones from the crumbling earth. At every pothole my friend yipped like a dog asleep till at last he jerked to with eyes that could've been eggs. When Super gave him the pipe, I thought he'd start coughing, but instead his face melted with the smoke from his lips.

"I was going to ask where we were," he said, "but now I don't even care. Onward, Benson!"

"We are no man's slave," Super said, and jerked his thumb aft, referring, I supposed, to the bed of broken dolls. "If you care to differ, interrogate the rest."

"I'm an army man, mister whatever-your-name-is," Dinky said.

"The name, boy, is Super."

"The way I said, Super," said Dinky, and drew himself up, "I'm an *army* man. And the only thing I'm good for is knowing what makes the grass grow green." He pointed at Super. "You know what makes the grass grow green?" he said. "Bright red blood."

"See what you know after you've been wearing that grass for a hat a few years."

"He's not always like this," I said.

Super let out a noise, maybe a chuckle, maybe not. "Oh, but you know he is," he said. "He's the marathon man. Catch our drift?"

"I am man!" Dinky shouted. "Hear me roar!"

In the distance a light appeared, I hadn't seen it off to the west as we came in—who lived out there? I thought, there's a light out there attached to nothing, it looked, a lonesome bulb in the trees—but then soon enough, like everything else, the question fell away, and when I looked up, we had reached our cabin.

The man turned his body and head in tandem. His mouth was an earwig, his eyes gleaming coins. "We'll be sorry to see you go."

"You don't have to go," Dinky said. "This is *our* place." Super fixed his gaze on my pal and said no more. "But we've got booze," Dinky said.

"We're a free man, boys, and wish you alike."

It must've been a good ten minutes we stood in the rain while Dinky worked to bring Super in, but the man evaded my friend until he had no choice but to turn away.

"There's nothing you can take from me," said Super when Dinky announced he'd take his leave, "but my life, but my life, but my life. Fortinbras!" he shouted at his dog. "It's time to make the soldiers shoot!"

Fortinbras appeared in the cab with his nose out the window, and the truck sputtered on. The last thing I saw was a sticker on the bumper. *I Have a Dream!*

WE STOOD IN THE RAIN, WATCHING BASIL through the window, berserk with his cherished knife. The freak never left without it, plus some rope and his grandfather's stupid hatchet, what, with the sack that held them, he called his *man-bag*. Every so often he'd mellow some, long enough to hypnotize whatever conjured fool had been dumb enough to block him. Then he spun off into the kicking, punching, and cutting he thought his moment of glory, the killing time. Well, the boob was dancing, and who could tell him otherwise?

Soundgarden was the band they'd picked to beat the ghosts. Hickory of course was what my eyes wanted, but they got Lucille—goddamn—snapping her fingers as she twirled. When finally Hickory did float up, Dinky fairly groaned. She was too lovely for her own good, it was true, and I was a fool in the rain.

"She's so beautiful," Dinky said.

"Lucy?" I said. "She's all right."

"Look at her," Dinky said. "She moves like… smoke."

"I don't know about you, but I am freezing."

Dinky wiped his nose. It could've been rotten fruit. "Basil won't be happy about his truck," he said. "He won't be happy at all."

My pal didn't look so hot. In fact my pal looked downright

fucked. "Basil," I said, "can gargle my nut sack. Let's go call you a doctor."

"Who do we think we are, always telling us what to do?"

"We think we're the guy who's smarter than the moron we're taking care of."

"Where's our bottle?"

"Milk's all gone, Dink," I said. "Diapers, too, in case you're wondering."

My friend glared like I'd stuck him with a shiv. "Have you ever chased a pig with a spear, AJ, then realized there was no pig?"

"What?" I said.

"Exactly," he said, and walked up the stairs.

SOMEONE HAD SET OUT THE CASE OF OLD CROW we'd brought, and the liter of Safeway coca-cola, all in a row with five new glasses. The rest lay spread across the table—CDs, lighters, bottle caps, shades, smoke packs empty and full, a half-munched bag of Chips Ahoy and a full one of Doritos, gum wrappers, peanut shells, matches, gum. Basil still had the knife, but now he had a bottle, too, stuck in his hole, what else. I thought he'd drain the thing for sure, but somehow he found the grace to pull up short and squirt an arc of whiskey through his teeth. Maybe fifteen bottles and cans lay about him, Lucky Lager, this round, with rebuses in their caps.

Hickory pointed at us the way children point at people who are fat. "They're here," she said.

Lucille ran outside, looking, I guessed, for the ice we'd never got.

"Some rabbits ran across the road," I said, and listened to the phone hum like a seashell at my ear.

"Where's my truck?" Basil said, moving in.

He did this sort of thing a lot, most recently to some pencil-necked kid at Radio Shack. At first the kid had given Basil hell for a mike cord he wanted to return. By the time we left, he'd freaked the kid so bad he had both his cord and a gift card worth ten bucks.

"We had an accident," Dinky said.

"An accident," Hickory said.

"This phone's shit the bed," I told them. "Is there another?"

Lucille, wet once again, had balled herself up in a chair by the hearth. Poor girl. The world wouldn't reckon like she'd been told.

"You blockheads," she said with tears in her eyes. "You're all a pack of blockheads." Dinky's nose was crusty with blood and snot. Anyone else would've been horrified just to see him. But these people, they didn't say a word. "All I wanted," Lucille said, "was a bag of ice."

Part of me had a craving to smack Lucille. Instead I knelt down before her. "Pretty often," I said, "it's hard to tell the difference between what hurts and what doesn't."

"I'm a sellout," she said. "A crappy, lousy sellout."

"I don't know about all that," Basil said. "I mean, you're just doing what you got to do."

"What would you know about it?"

"I work."

"At staying drunk you do. At schmoozing you do."

"Lucy," I said.

"You're wasting your time, AJ," Basil said. "Nothing you can do when she gets like this."

Lucille took up the *National Enquirer* at her feet and began to shred it. "How would you like to go around calling yourself, AJH vanden Heuvel, failed painter? AJH vanden Heuvel, CreditCom's newest Junior Project Analyst?"

"No one said you can't still do your thing," I said.

"Oh, joy. Yes, I'll give china-painting lessons Sunday afternoons. That'll do it."

I put a hand on her leg. "Have a beer," I said.

"I *know* what I am," she said. "It's just that I can't seem to help myself."

"People only think they know what they are."

"Yeah, well, I may not know all that, but what I think I know is that I'm a bitch."

"You hear that?" Basil said. "Mark that shit down."

"What I want to know," Lucille said, "is how life ever got to be so lovely and sweet."

The dead bird, its horrible stink, I couldn't get away…

I looked over my shoulder, and what should I see but two eyes staring from this poster, a cowgirl circa '75, with her fringed suede vest and denim blouse round the tits of the poster girl she was. She'd perked herself up against a pair of skis to smile toward the bedroom her smile let you know you'd soon be in… And now a shade's old song gamboled through my head, a poem I'd written way, way back, the worst… *a thousand wintry heaves ache beneath the sky… stop the whisper, recall the spring… when your shadow nears my blood, i sleep…*

"He needs a doctor," I said.

"Is he sick?" Lucille said.

"Is he sick."

"Are you sick, Dinky?" said Hickory. She'd got down beside him now and was stroking his arm.

"Look at him," I said. "I mean, Christ, you know?"

Basil drained a beer and flung the can. "Let's everybody look at poor Dinky." He wrinkled up his face and extended his hands like an impresario weary of his freak. "You'd think he's miserable. But the thing is, he likes it when crap goes sour."

"Are you actually putting *effort* into being such a dick?" Hickory said.

"All this attention he gets?" Basil said. "He's as happy as white on rice."

The tube meantime had been feeding us steady ruin—houses mired in water and mud; trees on roads; children clutching elders; stern-faced men, spent-faced men, some with slickers, others dusters, hauling sandbags and chattel; stranded vehicles and collapsing bridges; creatures mad with terror…

"AJ, baby," Basil said. "Bosom buddy. *Please.* Where the hell's my truck?"

"There was this rabbit," I said. "A guy gave us a ride."

"And who, pray tell, might that be?" Hickory said.

I told them about Super and his monkey. I told them about Fortinbras, and the little red Christ, and the truck of mangled dolls. Dinky stood up and shouted. He said how nervous we'd got when Super claimed to read our thoughts, how the geeze had ranted on about eagles and atomizers, the reversal of poles and the rest. Hickory asked if he was a shrink.

"He gave us drugs," Dinky said.

That got them frisky, all right.

"I'll tell you guys what," Basil said. "Maybe—and I mean just *maybe*—if you two morons get me really fucking baked, I'll forget you wrecked my truck."

I hadn't thought to query the old man whether he kept a stash for times he ran across dorks in the rain at night. That's what I said.

"So what was his name, then?" said Lucille.

"This you're not going to believe."

"Like I didn't already stop believing anything you say ten years back."

"He said it was Stuyvesant Something Something. Yeah. But he told us to call him Super."

Lucille said, "Next you'll be telling us he put a gun to your head and banged you in the heiny."

"Banged them in the ear, more like it," Basil said. "Knocked what was left of their rocks clean out."

Hickory said, "But wouldn't it be a marvel if he and Dinky were blood?"

Basil was pacing. "What are we going to do about my truck?" He poked Dinky's arm. "Cause in case you guys didn't know, good old shit for brains here was right for once in his life. The weatherman says it's going to flood like hell."

"Limo Wreck" became "The Day I Tried to Live." We gaped speechless at the phone till Hickory's sigh confirmed the real.

"We're stuck," she said.

Basil took up his knife. For a long time he gave us his back, running a thumb down the blade, but then he spun round and flung the thing at a pile of wood.

"You two morons are so lucky," he said after his knife had clattered to the floor. "I should skin you both, right here and now."

"You're lucky Granddad isn't here to skin *you*," Dinky said. "Granddad wouldn't like the way you're treating his place."

Lucille's face looked suddenly very stupid, like some girl about to get killed in a flick. "Did you hear that?" she said. No one said a word. "It was a voice," she said. "Like some horrible singing."

"You might remember, kids," Basil said, "there's something out there called a storm?"

"Sometimes, *squeeze*," Lucille said, "I think about what a bummer it is I'm not a man. I'd fuck you so hard you'd never—"

Subtle though it was, the sound repeated, just as Lucille had said, like some horrible singing. She went to the window—followed by me and Hickory and Basil with his hatchet—and moved from it to the next.

"Maybe it was a bear," she said after we'd covered the place for nothing.

Again Basil turned on her. "That's about as retarded as when you didn't know what a belly button is." This was true. At a lobster joint north of Ensenada, Lucille had downed a pitcher of booze and claimed belly buttons the stuff of shots at birth.

"Bears hibernate, Lucille," Dinky said.

"Yeah, well," Lucille said, grimacing at Basil, "at least I don't have a dick that hooks off thirty degrees right." She brushed a lock of hair from her face. "Fucking banana dick."

Now this was something not even I had ever heard. In all the time I'd known Basil, he'd never mentioned a faulty unit. "You're kidding," I said.

We all turned to the giant and watched his face screw up. He began to stutter, but that didn't work either, so he poured himself a drink.

"Anyway," he said, "there's nothing out there."

"There's nothing out there *now*," Hickory said.

"Who's your closest neighbor?" I said.

"We don't have neighbors," Dinky said. "We've got fences."

"Turn out the lights," I said.

"Fuck you," Basil said.

"So we can see what's out there."

Again we peered out the window, looking for shapes, a car, a ghost, whatever, but found the same old rain and trees in the same old howling night, the same uncanny sense of possibilities imminent.

"The wind can do some batty shit," Basil said, and raised his glass in a toast. "Here's to Buddy Time."

Hickory stood close against me, jungle sweet, the smell of her strong, cucumber and vanilla. Her hand covered mine, she smiled, my hand was in hers, my hand was in her hand. I wanted to eat her teeth, then. I wanted to climb inside her, tired and full, and fall into precious sleep.

"Days like this," she said, "they say *damn the water and burn the wine.*"

"Sounds to us," Dinky said, "a bit like that *seize the day* crap everyone's been spouting."

Lucille picked up *Fear and Loathing*. "'We had two bags of grass,' she said, reading from the cover, 'seventy-five pellets of mescaline, five sheets of high-powered blotter acid, a salt shaker half-full of cocaine and a whole galaxy of multicolored uppers, downers, screamers, laughers and also a quart of tequila, a quart of rum, a case of Budweiser, a pint of raw ether, and two dozen amyls.' Is that cool or what?" she said, and tossed the book down.

"Everyone knows Hunter S is our hero," Dinky said. "His work with the Hell's Angels was nothing short of revolutionary."

"Now that," Basil said, "I'll give you."

"They even put a contract out on him for it. Who's that Indian fellow, Rushdie or whoever the heck?" Dinky turned away to cough. "Excuse us," he said, wiping his mouth with an arm. "The guy the Ayatollah wants offed? An *ant*. A literary microbe squirming in the shadow of the god." He shuffled over and held out the book like the Bible itself. "'He who makes a beast of himself,' he said, quoting from the epigraph, 'gets rid of the pain of being a man.'" He took a moment to stare us down. "Hunter S," he said, "showed us all who we really are."

"I got to give it to you one more time, Dink," Basil said, slapping him on the back. "You poor fuckless fart."

"Hey you guys," Hickory said. "Guess what?"

"What?" Basil said.

"Lick my butt!" Hickory said, and burst out laughing. She was whacking on her knee like some old gal from Arkansas. "No, but seriously. Anybody here ever play Truth or Dare?"

"We won't play," Dinky said, "but we'll sure watch." He

beamed at Hickory and made an effort to grin. "We *like* to watch."

Hickory led Lucille to the center of the room and plopped down on the floor. "Come along now, Basil darling," she said. "We're dying to know your secrets."

Basil scratched his balls. "I like a good dare every now and then. Keeps me on my toes."

"Bring the hooch," I said, "and whatever else."

"Perchance we could change the music?" Hickory said. "And that abominable machine as well," she said, indicating the TV. "Please."

"'4th of July,'" Basil said, "is one of the great all-timers."

"Try the Jelly Roll Morton."

Some talk went round how the old master thought a Haitian witch had cursed him. Dinky, back on the couch, said that in the end Jelly Roll had taken to acting like Howard Hughes.

"The guy never ventured out," he said. "And nobody cursed him, either. He'd simply trapped himself in his own little cage of fear. At least that's our view. For what it's worth."

"Break out the Jelly Roll, *squeeze*!"

"Damn it, woman," Basil said. "How many times do I have to tell you not to call me that in public?"

Lucille squinted. "This is public?"

WE'D MET HICKORY AT A PARTY IN THE CITY. TO get inside, you had to take an ancient lift, the kind with a platform behind a metal door that wouldn't budge without a couple of trolls to heave on some old chain. They even had a bellhop, in a red-velvet monkey suit and pillbox hat with a strap. For eyebrows the kid had little steel barbells, five or six per side, and for teeth real fangs, straight-up Lestat. And if that weren't enough, he was running Maori-style ink on his chin, and every patch of his face but that was goofy with shiny dust.

Before us lay a massive room, probably two- or three-hundred yards long and half as wide, chockful with every type of gork in the book. Guys with bunless chaps ran around the place smacking each other with crops. Chicks, too, more than half of them decked out like Catwoman, scampered about with nipple clamps and whips and chains, wreaking all manner of hell. There were go-go dancers in bubbles and cages, Rastafaris, homeboys, deathrockers and mods, rockabilly kids, swingers and punks, not to mention your basic Haight Street hipsters. Jumbotrons swayed from the ceilings flashing clever retromercials, and thrift-store TVs lined the walls fuzzy with chickens in the slaughterhouse and Japanimation and big-time sex acts, the whole of it swamped in banks of chemical fog. Some heavy-duty industrial house provided the coup de grâce for this late-night get down, pumping so hard you could feel it from the marrow in your bones to the depths of your aching nards. The four of us snagged some drinks and split, the two traitors one way, Dinky and I the next.

We stumbled on our girl in some sort of cave, everyone but her stupid with dope. In her tight corduroys and glittering boots, she sat among thirty or forty crackpot fiends sucking fingers, faces, toes, whatever their mouths could hold. But what stung most was the guy beside her, an image to the T of my old toad in a picture I'd seen when he was a Hare Krishna. He had fierce blue eyes and a queue from his head, all the way down his back. He was even wearing bamboo thongs. Soon, however, he slipped off, and I forgot him and was glad. Jerks by the droves kept trying to get their paws on Hickory, but she sat among them cool as a queen, there, as she'd said, "to take in all the footage." We never asked her name, and she never said. It was Dinky laid the moniker down. "You look like a Hickory girl if ever we've seen one," he told her, to which she said, "Hickory dickory dock, the mouse ran up the clock." All the while her face lay before us unreadable as Chinese kanji. I remember staring at her for a preposterously long time, asking myself just who in hell this willow was, with the ovate eyes and strong white teeth, and me like a doofus trying to smile.

So I'd known what I wanted before the game had begun. The problem was, having so much to want, I had to choose.

"What's your name?" I said. "Your *real* name."

No one but Dinky would've expected that. Neither Basil nor Lucille had ever known Hickory wasn't Hickory. The day we introduced her, it was *Hickory, meet Basil and Lucille.* Their faces didn't quite know what to do.

"I've always wondered," Hickory said, "why none of you have asked."

"It can't be more fucked up than Hickory," Basil said.

"Elmira Pugsley?" Hickory said.

"It's different," Lucille said. "That's for sure."

"It's after my granny. But since the point here's to be totally honest—and I'm a totally honest gal—the full name's Elmira Beatrice Pugsley."

Basil clicked his tongue. "Poor, *poor* girl," he said.

"No wonder you go around letting everyone call you Hickory," Lucille said.

Dinky burbled from the couch. "We don't think that's very nice, now do we?"

"Who asked you to wake up, hey moron?" Basil said.

"The middle name," Hickory went on, "that was my father's doing. They were farmer hippies."

"You," I said, "come from *hippies*?"

Hickory smiled. "I spent the first ten years of my life on a commune up in Oregon. We had beehives and everything. Organic bees. Organic everything."

"Poor, poor girl," Basil said.

Hickory put her chin in her palm and looked us over. When she stopped at me I knew what she wanted, but then she passed to Basil. "You, tough guy. Which will it be?"

"Toss a mop on the floor," I said at Basil's show of squirming. "See which way it flops."

Even as I said this it struck me just how much we didn't care what Basil did. We knew—or at least I knew, or thought I knew—that either way he turned wouldn't change a thing. How could he choose when he had no choice, the difference between a Truth or Dare having collapsed beneath their emptiness? For Basil, to be honest meant to be daring. And however strangely, however sadly, daring was as close as Basil ever got to truth. The notions had become two mirrors reflecting only themselves.

"Goddamn it," Basil said. "*Shit.* Truth."

"Oh dear yes, quite lovely indeed," Hickory said in this high-society debutante voice. "Now. What's the most shameful thing you've ever done—sexually, I mean?" Basil looked blank, so Hickory said, "Of course I mean shameful in the traditional sense, the sub*urban* sense."

"I can tell you *that*," Lucille said. "It happened only last week, when he greased me up like a Thanksgiving turkey and tried to—"

"I already heard that story," I said. Lucille turned with gaping eyes. "He told me *every*thing," I said.

"Everything?" she said.

Basil cleared his throat. "When I was a kid," he said, "I had a stuffed monkey."

"How old are we talking?" Hickory said.

"Twelve or thirteen, I guess. My dad had given it to me before he took off. Anyways, it had this hole in its crotch. It started out little, but kept getting bigger." Basil had been slouching forward as he talked. Now he planted his hands on the floor, as if the telling were over.

"What kind of story is that?" I said.

Basil's face was flushing now. "There's more," he said.

"Come, come," Hickory said.

"One day I was in the closet."

"Yes?"

"With the monkey."

"Yes?"

"And I was looking at pornos, you know, and, I don't know, there it was." Here Basil paused with great melodrama, worse than a creep on the tube.

"Out with it!" I shouted.

"So I fucked it."

"Really?" Lucille said, her face lit up.

"That's not all," Basil said.

"There's more," I said. "There's always more with this guy."

"See, when I finished, I wanted to hide the bastard, but I couldn't think of any place where my ma wouldn't find it. There was also another lady and her kid living with us in this house. You can see why I had to destroy the facts. So I got out a big old garbage bag, one of those super heavy-duty Glad bags, and stuffed the monkey in there. Then I jumped on my moped and drove out to the mall. They had all those dumpsters in the alley behind the Mervyns there. Thing is, I didn't just chuck it in there. I *buried* it. Dug through old tampons and shit, and chicken bones and diapers and soup cans, all that repugnant shit, and crammed that little fucker down at the very, very bottom, and then I covered it all back up."

"You *interred* it," Hickory said. "As in a mausoleum." Now she circled our faces with a look that said *I'm going to tell you all what this really means.* "Some people would say that was very symbolic."

"Not this again," Lucille said.

"I fucked a stuffed monkey," Basil said. "Big deal."

"First of all," Hickory said, "it wasn't just any old monkey. It was the monkey your *father* gave you before he *abandoned* you. That's why you killed the monkey. You *fucked* it, as you say. And then, because you couldn't live with the guilt, you buried it someplace where no one would ever find it."

"You," Basil said, "are a goddamned fruit loop."

"Check out the science," Hickory said.

"Ha!" Lucille said.

"Seriously," Hickory said. "I'm not surprised in the least. It was a very normal thing to do for a boy that age. Especially in our culture. He just did it in an abnormal way."

Dinky rolled up on an elbow and scratched his chest. "You know what Hermann Goering said about our culture? He said, 'When I hear anyone speak of culture, I reach for my revolver.'"

"*You're* the one belongs in the loony bin," I told Basil. He had a big whitehead on his nose I'd just noticed. "I'll bet you even crammed that thing full of mayonnaise before you did it."

"It's all right, baby," Lucille said, rubbing his back. "I still love you."

"We think we'll be going upstairs now," Dinky said. "We're going to lie down for a while." He stood there in his Cal Bears rugby shirt and Joe Boxer boxers with their bologna-sandwich appliqués. Then he sniffled and wiped his nose and started away, dragging his feet like they were a couple of sleds. "We don't suppose any of you would care to tuck us in?"

"I'd love to oblige," Lucille said, "but I know how you get when a bed's nearby."

"Not that I'd worry so much about that," Basil said. His face was waxy now, a veneer of cosmopolite ugly. "He ain't exactly what I'd call, you know, at the height of his form these days."

Dinky picked his nose. Then, his face a model of serenity, he extended his arm and with a simple motion of thumb and finger flicked the booger onto Basil's hat. "At least our dick is straight," he said, looking at Lucille.

"That thing better not have landed on me," Basil said. "I'll cut that straight dick off. Go ahead," he said, "go to sleep. But beware."

"I knew a guy," I said, "who woke up one morning and went to take a pee, and when he pulled his dick out, guess what color it was?"

"You guys are so sick," Hickory said. "I'm trapped in a shack with a grade-A bunch of sickos."

"Black," I said. "As your crappy gaping pupils, I'm talking."

"In fact, to call you nothing but sickos is a kindness you scarcely deserve."

"Turns out," I said, "the guy had got so blotto he didn't even know his frat buddy'd taken the thing out in the middle of the night and colored it with a Magic Marker, one of those big-ass felt-tipped Magic Markers with the refillable cartridges even."

"I find a booger on me," Basil said, "I'll cut his dick off."

"Come on, Dinky," Hickory said. "You go lie down, and I'll make you some tea."

Dinky left. We could hear him shuffling up the stairs and across the floor above. No one said anything to Basil about the booger on his hat. We just poured more drinks.

"Sometimes," Basil said, "I think, *Man, that guy's got no spine at all.*"

"Character," Lucille said. "He's got no character."

"No, I mean *spine*. Character'd be what you are. And you're only what you are when the lights go down."

"The guy's been a year in Bosnia," I said. "Sleeping in two feet of mud. Eating Ball Park Franks and Twinkies and shit."

"We all know he didn't go over there because he's a patriot."

"If you were into ninety grand of debt," I said, "and didn't have a way to pay it off, you'd've joined the army, too."

"Dinky joined the army because it's not the *real world*. Like everything else he does. To keep from doing anything *real*, I mean. Like a real job. Like a career."

Hickory snorted. "What, and you call driving around HelLA a couple hours a day a career? You call that a *job* even, chucking papers on the curb?"

"He wouldn't even do that," I said, "if he didn't feel so guilty for a life's worth of mooching off his sugar units."

"Bitch," said Basil. "I'm a professional musician."

"You're a record company's bagboy."

"I'm the mother fucking mover and shaker who's going to make your ass pay, is what I am. And guess what else? It's only a matter of time."

"You're thirty-five years old, Basil. You know as well as those record people do the kiddies won't be lining up to see your teeth fall out. Not to mention you could stop kicking everybody out of your band all the time."

"So I'll be fat and bald and toothless, but at least I'll be up there. Sure as hell beats chasing pubes for a living."

"That's not *even* cool."

"You want to be cool, be cool."

"Look, you boobs," Lucille said, "are we still playing or what?"

There was that briefest moment of doubt where Basil and I considered exchanging our knives for guns or throwing the knives away. But really the doubt was feigned. We knew what would happen. The kill was just a dream. The sight of blood was enough. We were only after the blood. This of course was a perversion cultivated over time, like a taste for taboo food, monkey brain or mice. The satisfaction of knowing we'd wounded one another was more than sufficient. In fact, it had become for us a fix of sorts, why our hate for one another always equaled our need. Basil and I were Siamese twins parted only in flesh.

"Hell yes, we are," he said, "and it's still my turn."

"Your turn?" Hickory said.

"To ask."

Lucille tossed back a shot. "Well ask away then," she said. "Ask away the doo-da day."

BASIL WASN'T GOING TO ASK LUCILLE ANYTHING worth her breath. He already thought he knew everything she had to say, a presumption which, so far as I could tell, was nowhere near the facts. And whereas it was true that before she'd become his woman he wouldn't have thought twice about crushing her at every meal, now that she was his, he'd save his curiosity for the pillow talk to come.

I was absolutely positive, for instance, he didn't know a thing about the times my ex-wife and I found the cupboards full of empty cereal boxes those three months Lucille had crashed our sofa. And if not cereal boxes, it was milk cartons at the back of the fridge, dry, or garbage cans stuffed with candy bar wrappers and foils from TV dinners. An entire roast would've vanished in the night, or a pot of spaghetti we'd just made, or a half-gallon of ice cream, all manner of food all of the time. Basil didn't know, either, how those very mornings, I'd enter the bathroom to the odor of Lysol and vomit.

And neither would Basil ask why Lucille had slept with each of the three Gladden brothers that crazy summer of '87, when after munching three grams of shrooms and a hit of blotter our friend Moo-Moo stumbled through a skylight and broke his legs; when our dealer Tony the Tongue invited four girls to the House of Men for a session of free love only to fake an epilepsy fit after two of the vixens tried to pork him with their strap-ons; when in front of the Grand Lake Theater a herd of cops arrested me and Dinky and Basil for having bombed a woman with a fire extinguisher just because she looked, as Basil claimed, like Barney Rubble with tits: while she went ape shit and chased us howling, we burned rubber through a KFC lot full of cops gathered for an ad lib feast. They caught us with three fat blunts, a bottle of wine, and a BB gun, fully loaded.

But Lucille. First she'd taken Bobby, then Benjamin, then Brad. Not one of these brothers knew the rest were boofing her, too. Because with the mornings, with the rising of suns and fungus-eyed friends—whichever friends happened to've been in whatever house she and the brother-at-hand had done their boofing in—Lucille would appear all by her lonesome in the crumpled state she'd adopted as style. Back then, the girl wore nothing but Birkenstock sandals and macramé anklets, cutoff Levi's or OshKosh overalls smeared with the paint of her artistic dabblings—an imitative blend of Arthur Dove and Marsden Hartley with a hint of Homer's seascapes—them and her Grateful Dead tees, tie-dyed, of course. When the weather was bad, she'd wear some Tijuana poncho and often even a blanket round her neck, like some queen-of-People's-Park swaddled in mangy ermine. And this was on top of her feeble attempt at sprouting a noggin full of dreads. The day would begin like habit, bong hits all around, the morning's wine in homemade mugs. Whichever Gladden brother she'd been with had already slipped through the woodwork like the creeping ferret he was, so that when all was said and done, that, as they say, was that.

Later, after these affairs had caved, we began to crush Lucille with gossip. And though for the next few years shadows kept the details grey, the matter cohered vaguely nonetheless. That's how these things work: one morning, said Misha, who'd got the scoop from Lisa, who'd pinched it from her boy Sam, whom Bobby himself had told, Bobby bragged about the compliments his lovers all gave his beautiful cock, which, according to Lisa-by-way-of-Karen-by-way-of-Lucille, was hardly the case; as for Brad—Lucille's last of the brothers—he had caught the clap (someone else had slipped between him and Ben); and Ben had a girl in the east who'd found out about his slick business, then told another friend, who, of course—because, again, that's the way these things go down—was a friend of mine.

And where I was concerned, what could Basil ask he didn't already know? How many diseases I'd got by the time I hit twenty, or had I shoplifted as a kid or tinkered with sex? The closest it came to that was kissing my cousin when I was five, beneath a blanket on Christmas Eve. Though my dear old toad had no doubt caught us, he was kind enough to wait till morning, dressed like a Hare Krishna elf, to beat me with his paddle.

Nor would Basil ask why I'd called last year at four a.m. to say something was amiss with his granny. She'd just suffered a lapse in health he and his mom went nutty for, some sort of brain hemorrhage I knew nothing of. At the time I considered my little call a motiveless joke spawned by a five-day binge during which I'd consumed three eight balls, seven quarts of bourbon, five cases of sucky beer, and nineteen or twenty packs of smokes—and that's forgetting my jaunt through Berkeley's midnight streets in nothing but a beanie with a propeller on top, ranting about Ezekiel's wheels gleaming of beryl and the predictions of Nostradamus.

But later, in the clarity of my regret, I saw the canker in the bloom. Basil had "fired" me (that was the expression he used once he started talking smack) from what he obviously had considered "his" band. In a dull autumn noon veined with dull autumn smog, we sat over a mound of pad thai and confessed our interests had suffered a rift. He felt, or so he said, I could do better elsewhere. Get out on my own maybe, he'd been stifling my creativity and such, he said. But even in the midst of these shams we both knew he was wonking through his bullshit tulips, making a farce of protecting my ego while disguising the rage of his own.

That he knew I knew he knew I knew all this made it the more obscene. His head had grown bigger even than Dinky's, which wasn't to say my own had shrunk. I'd risen from the glop of my tyro swamp, having begun my apprenticeship in music just five years back. Now a producer chose my song from a group of twenty-plus that Basil and I'd mostly co-written, claiming it the stuff of hits. But that didn't justify anyone calling me greedy, not like they could Basil. The cat couldn't share a stinking thing—not money, not women, not smokes, not booze, not cars, not drugs, not *nada*. Why the hell would he share the title Creative Genius—whatever that meant: more groupie sex? a solo name-drop in the *Chronicle*'s Pink Section or *BAM* magazine?—even though he'd already taken all but the glamor-light itself with his singing and playing both? People by then were comparing him to stars like Paul Westerberg and Chris Cornell and Sting. Did that matter? Not a stewed red penny. A shadow's shadow threatened the kid. The shadow itself nigh on crushed him. And the thing that made the shadow, when it came too near, it might as well have been King Kong. We sat there stabbing at our shrimps, hoping the waiter would bring us the check so we could go get drunker than we were.

And the more I thought, the more seeds of deviance I scraped up. In our high school days, Basil's grandparents left each year for a three-month tour to Europe or wherever, leaving us to our bashes at their mansion in the hills. It was during their last trip, before his grandpa died, that I got plastered on

Rainier Ale. I was sixteen years old, shorter and skinnier than I am today, a gawky, graceless runt, for sure, in size five-and-a-half waffle stompers and a Gor-Tex parka stuffed with paraphernalia and drugs, and long, greasy hair, and zits the size of gumballs. Between my having left the party and gained the john, I'd become so drunk that when finally I began to hurl I lost control and shit my pants. And this was no ordinary shitting, either, nothing like a few solid logs you could scrape into the bowl and have done. We were talking about a sloppy, repulsive mess, full of chilidogs and Funyuns and Hostess Apple Pie, to say nothing of all that brew, an honest-to-god shitting if ever a shitting was. Really, I should've been proud of that dump, but I was a twerp. It made the Montezuma's Revenge in some tripper's shorts look like a painting by Renoir, green and yellow and slimy as it was, running down my legs and the pants at my ankles and even in my boots. To make matters worse—if that were possible—a very special girl had come that night, a little vixen with whom I fancied myself in love. For months I'd been chasing her eye, going so far as to write her a poem she wasted no time laughing at with her friends on the quad. Had I merely barfed, I'd've been okay. But I had to go and crap my pants, and that no one could pardon. So there I stood moaning and crying and retching in the shower, and when I called Basil to ask for a pair of trunks, what did he do but burst out cackling. Because that was the kind of guy Basil was. He made buffoonery of your heroics and heroics of your buffoonery. If you told a joke, he made it your inexcusable flaw. You had a flaw, he turned it to a nasty joke. After laughing till he cried, my dear buddy rushed out to the PA for his band. "Hey, everybody!" he yelled at the mike. "Guess what? AJ just crapped his pants!"

Another time, high on mesc, Basil lit some kid's hair on fire just because it looked, as Basil said, *like it would burn real good.*

Another time yet he turned me in to the dean after the dean had caught us smoking dope in the bushes behind the portables. I'd run down the hill and got away clean while Basil and the other tard with us stayed put like the dean had said. Basil never knew I was the one who'd slashed his tires the night he fell asleep in his van after banging some girl he'd dragged from The Ivy Room. Basil never found out, either, how I'd filled the lock to his apartment with glue. He was living in a rat hole near West Oakland, whose landlord hated to answer his phone. Wearing his clothes for the days it took Basil to get inside pounded him with jock itch.

The one person Basil could demand a real Truth or Dare from was Hickory, the only one he hadn't known for more than half his life. I listened to the howling rain while Jelly Roll Morton bopped on the ivories and Lucille tore open some Mexican candy bar I'd never seen, with a load of marshmallow and other shit that looked like blood. I thought how when it rained my old toad would tell me the undertaker's wife was coming to take me away. He and moms had so many ways of expressing their love. *Every time you sigh*, moms used to say, *you lose a drop of blood, and that just keeps bringing you closer to death.* Then she'd sigh, and I would scream, *O Mama, Mama, Mama!* while she and my toad fell back laughing. I thought about all the creatures in this wintry world, out where the rocks lay cold and the mud ran thick and the trees and wind and clouds sputtered and racked and rolled, and Basil sat there before me with his impudence and his flaws and his knowledge of and persistence in them. He took great pleasure in these traits. They somehow gave him the sense he'd become indispensable to the people on whom he committed his tiny crimes, the way delusions become vital to the hypochondriac. His face was always glistening with that petty smirk of self-awareness. Even in his antagonism he'd become precious to those he knew—big, goofy, confident, fashionable, dear, droll Basil, the helpmeet fright wig, twentieth-century portrait of Juvenalian adage—two things only the people anxiously desire: bread and circuses. God, how I hated that I loved him. And then there was Hickory lounging in the smoke with her ink-black hair and creamy throat while upstairs Dinky wheezed among his dreams.

"I should ask her," Basil said, as I had guessed, sneering Hickory's way. The booger was still lodged in his hat. "But I won't. You, doofus," he said to me, "Truth or Dare. And don't give us another one of your boring-ass stories we've all heard a jillion times."

Across the room our bottles sang their nitwit song. I'd talked to them in the past, my bottles, and held them close. "Sweet, sweet booze," I'd say, "please don't ever leave me." I crawled to the table and stuck one in my mouth.

"Truth," I said.

"We want to hear more about your fucked up family."

"Yeah," Lucille said. "Tell us more about your Hare Krishna dad."

I smiled my smile of the hero, the general at his table of defeat, surrendering up his troops.

"I ever tell you my old toad was a paperboy?"

"Every kid was a paperboy," Lucille said.

"I mean when he was forty-two."

I told them how after he'd quit the Hare Krishna's, no place would hire him, no place real. He still had that bald head with the queue down his back. Who was going to hire a guy that looked like soap-on-a-rope? He delivered those worthless inserts with the advertisements in them, I explained, the ones with the Round Table Pizza coupons and Thrifty's discount ads and such.

But what I did not tell them was how my whole life it seemed I had to watch my ass, waiting for that fuck to sneak up and holler: *Andrew Jackson!*

What I did not tell them was how he would jump, and I'd run, and bit by bit the time would pass until he caught me with his paddle.

What I did not tell them was how from the shadows my mother would always laugh. *Yes*, she'd say, *yes*...

And for absolutely positively certain what I did not tell them was every time he saw me my grandfather said how he and dear ma had spoiled my mother past sense. They may've had to scratch it out, but that never kept them from giving her love. He gave her love sure, he'd say, especially him, more than she could use. Their lives, he said, were each other. On their wedding day, when they and theirs and all theirs too came dusting through the gates to the fields trying to swallow up the house for the last hundred years, the place was a vision or mirage. They spat from barrels and slapped on legs and pebbled the hens and drank from a bottomless jug. And the goods, he said, did they ever have them: black-eyed peas, corn bread and greens, pickled peaches, and okra, and ham. Greasy fingers ran through tri-tip and pone, gravy and spuds and coleslaw, too, and laughing mouths scarfed cookies and apple pie. If the men weren't eating or drinking in tens, and the women weren't doing the same, it's because they were together. They hooted into that Texas night, he said, and no one cried unless for good. In the morning, for their honeymoon, they chugged on down to Austin. He spoke about those times like they'd just passed, my grandfather did, their five wild nights in the honkytonks and jukes and once a hall with its giant band, the champagne swilling and they screwing like bugs wherever they could—on the hay-riddled planks of the '29 Ford, in the alleys with the tramps and garbage and toms, but mostly in their eight-bit bed—all this before returning to the dust of the fields and the everyday sun. Lucky for grandy she couldn't make more after whelping out moms, my grandfather said. *She all but dried up, like a row of set alfalfa.* Of course the coot presumed he'd done what he could to make sure moms knew he loved her. He never could see how once she'd grown to bleed she didn't want him anymore, he said, why she went away. And the day he himself went away, I drove off with my old toad and moms to gather what he'd left of grandy in Lamesa. Not so, however, the day my own toad croaked. The first thing I did was strip an ambulance clean and smash it all to bits. It was only later someone told me I'd done every crumb of dope I stole before they'd fed my toad to the grave, how everything stunk of ether and mints. *Red rover, red rover, send happiness over*—that's what the voices said. And then it was them on the street, plotting my destruction, bearded women, first, then barkers and trolls, then geeks and elves and clowns would come to lay me siege. Robitussin low balls and speed-jacked marys made my fare. Sometimes I drank water, sometimes I even slept. We buddies went to jerks with names we didn't know and watched films whose stories were an endless blur. And sometimes, like now, we journeyed on trips whose ends we'd never guess...

For a long while no one said a word. That stood to sense. The only thing we knew was how to keep on boozing. And my dear friends, I trusted, wouldn't—couldn't—ever feel the emptiness of that, leastwise not how I did. We couldn't go forever. Sooner or later we'd have to lie down in darkness. Without the speed that had kept us hopping, I saw no other way. Any time now we'd collapse around the secrets of ourselves, the ones we knew and the ones we didn't.

I was tired of believing a shroud could mute the sense that some dimly feared disaster might beset me in the night. Let it come. It couldn't be more terrifying than sleep, with its dreams realer than our lives. The party was ending, that was sure. We'd torn our gifts open to find boxes inside boxes inside boxes, and nothing in the last. Good riddance, holidays—*sayonara*.

"I forgot Dinky's tea," Hickory said at last, and glided toward the kitchen. "I'll just make him a cup of tea."

"What're you going to make it with, pine cones?"

Basil was right. Everything we had was on the table.

"Think I'll go see what's up with army boy myself," I said.

"Check the phone while you're at it," Basil said. "Maybe it's working now."

But when still nothing but fuzz dribbled from the thing, Basil flung his hatchet at the stack of wood and cracked his knuckles like he did when he was tight, a tic I'd grown to hate across the years, not for its sound but what it foretold: my bosom pal was about to become a bigger asshole yet.

"Next thing you know," he said, "we'll be eating each other for breakfast like the losers in the Donner Party." He dug his fingers into Lucille's ass and lurched at her with fangs. "My oh my how these buttocks are sweet," he said. "Fingergoddamnedlickinggood they are, oh my, oh my."

"That's not funny," Hickory said.

"This isn't funny?"

"What you said. It wasn't funny."

"But her ass does taste good." Basil held a hand over Lucille's butt. "See for yourself."

"It's just not funny, talking about our predicament that way. Even as a joke."

I was surprised at Basil's little fun. He had his man-bag with its hatchet and knife and rope for good reason, or for reason good for him. Territory past any town's limit was territory rife with *Deliverance*-type freaks and fools gone native, full of conspiracy theories and tales of a world destroyed—with fruitcakes, essentially, like Super. Every time we hit Baja, much less the Berkeley Hills, Basil would forage through the mess in his truck to make sure he had his kit. It didn't matter the fun we made. He'd just tell us to thank him when we're old, for our necks from the noose that day back when. And the Donner Party especially. I don't know how many times he'd spun yarns about it, like tales from the crypt, bemoaning, at bottom, their fates as fodder for themselves. The notion he'd end his days in someone else's stomach was for him the doomsday to beat all doom ever. The man couldn't see three frames of a zombie flick without breaking into hives. Watching him blow his top was always a gas. Every now and then, just to flip his wig the way I knew it would, I'd break out the drumstick from a turkey or chicken and cackle like hell while the fantods rocked him. If he was joking about the Donner Party now, it meant one thing: he was scared.

"I'm sorry," Basil said. "It just seemed like a good time to throw caution to the wind."

Hickory gave him two numb eyes, then went to the CD player and dropped in *Murder Ballads*, by Nick Cave and his Seeds. A ghost-cold bass sauntered from the speakers, and then that guitar's staccato chook, the piano leaping at every fourth while the reverb spread like a stain…

*So he walked through the rain,*
*and he walked through the mud*
*till he came to a place called The Bucket of Blood—*
*Stagger Lee!*

I'D JUST SCANNED AN AD FOR A DILDO INSIDE Dinky's latest trash, *Pink Champagne Bitch*, when a turmoil of voices called me back.

"I'm telling you," Lucille shouted, "someone's out there!"

Dinky must have heard it, too. He lurched up hideous and swollen and said, "That's our book… Turn out the lights… No…" Then he cocked an ear to the door. "Who invited her?"

"I came in to check on you," I said.

"In the dream I was having…" I waited for him to go on about this dream but his words were dribble.

"In the dream you were having what?"

Dinky covered his face with the sheet and coughed. "Maybe we could ask those chuckleheads to put a lid on it. Do you think we could do that, Andrew?"

From the wall above him a clown gazed out with that comically lugubrious expression old people somehow feel compelled to adorn the faces of clowns in art. Dinky's great-goddamned-grandmother, or someone like her, had probably slapped it up.

"Even if I wanted to," he said, and looked away, "I couldn't." I watched him fumble with his pants. He looked like a child, with a child's confessional eyes. "Hickory, I mean," he said, though I'd known what he meant. His lips were trembling. He was speaking of himself as *I*. "I only wanted someone to hold," he said. I realized then the clown was staring at me, too, or so it seemed. I hated clowns more than anything, to say nothing of paintings of clowns. And now Dinky had to go and lay a guilt trip out. "About getting her on her back. You know I didn't mean it… Right?" His hands came up as if with a toxic globe. "Look at me," he said. I tried to look out the window but only saw myself. "How can a guy get any sleep with that?"

We heard Basil say, "Turn out the lights," and then Hickory something about a lamp. Meanwhile Lucille had begun to chant: "O my God O my God O my God."

The sounds were undeniable, clunky and deep at first, like a hammer on a hollow box, scratchy and thin the next. By the time we reached them, Hickory, Basil, and Lucille were at the window again, with just their eyes above the sill.

"Watch it, you guys," Lucille said. "Someone's out there."

"No one's out there," Basil said.

Dinky slid down the jamb and turned into a ball. "Is that why we're all on our hands and knees?"

"There," Lucille said, and pointed. "Did you see that?"

For just this once I wished she'd been lying, but she had seen what she'd seen. A shadow moved through the rain, then faded into mist. Then the sounds began again, leisurely nearly, steady, like a bridge troll, or maybe a giant, crunching on his bones.

"Who do you think it is?" I whispered.

On a talk show on the tube three enormous women argued round a little man while the singer from his box moaned about a girl with hair full of ribbons and gloves on her hands.

"You're out of your mind," Basil said. "I didn't see dick."

"Someone *is* out there," I said.

"Then that's it," Basil said, and strode to the door with his hatchet. "I go out there and holler, and no one answers, I don't care if it's the Queen of fucking England, when I see him, he's as dead as fuck. What's the matter, baldy?" he said when Dinky wouldn't budge. "Afraid of the big bad wolf?"

"The guy can hardly walk," I said.

"He's good enough to get out of bed, he's good enough to kick some ass."

"Blood," Dinky mumbled. "Bright red blood."

"Don't do it," Hickory said.

Lucille began to wail, something I couldn't get.

Basil glared. "You coming or not?"

We went into that fist of night, hunched against the rain, scared as hell, too, speaking for myself. Something was out there, in the wallows beneath the deck perchance, lurking and munching, and we were stoned and drunk and tired, to say nothing of critically blind. I looked to Hickory above me, her hand on Dinky's arm. The best my friend could do was prop himself up to watch. By the way she cradled him, I could tell it was all for show. She wanted him to think she thought he needed checking. The rain had soaked me through again, now. I felt dirty and soft and stupid as could be.

Basil moved crabwise down the stairs, brandishing the hatchet. "Whoever you are," he said, "you'd better stop fucking around, cause we mean business."

Once upon a time I'd fancied myself that bearded miser's secret spy for truth—*once upon a time.* Because now we were stuck in a game. Anything could happen, anything at all.

"After we go around," I said, "you stick to the wall, and I'll slip over by the trees. That way, whoever it is, if he's got a gun, he can't get both of us at once."

"Where's my knife?"

The water ran down our faces, over the brim of Basil's hat, his face a glistening shade. I could see his hatchet. I could see his shiny teeth.

"There's this," I said, and showed him my Swiss Army pocketknife.

"You *little* fuck," he said.

I stepped toward the trees, trying to keep my footing in the mud. Basil crept along the wall until a thick, hollow *cloonk* sounded through the pitch, and then a muffled *humph*. He had plunged to the ground and by the time I reached him was rocking to and fro.

"Son of a bitch of a stone slammed me in the balls, man."

Again we heard the sounds, this time from inside the cabin. My brain was reeling, with gutter rags and dirty socks, and broken teeth, and fingers, and brooms.

"He's in the basement," I said.

"I heard the bastard."

I tried to take his hatchet. "Maybe you should give me that."

"The hell you will."

My buddies at the window couldn't see us or anything else. They couldn't hear a thing, either—nothing but wind and rain. All they could do was wait, afraid for the sound of a shot, the screams of some twit getting killed. I squinted hard at the trees as their skin crept round their Etch A Sketch limbs, searching endlessly it seemed for the lamest of signs, until just as I was ready to quit a shape emerged from the wall at my right, about twenty feet off, and like a phantom set our way.

"There he is!" I said.

Basil leapt growling to his feet and drove toward the shape, its movements clipped, as if by a wound. The shape came on, a man now, I knew, who might not've seen us even, lurching as he was to some alien poise. But just as Basil fell on him, the man feinted one way and dodged the next. The hatchet made an arc of whaleback-blue, then dropped wide of the man, and the man leapt forward and spun and with a boot sent Basil down. Then both fell from sight but as quickly emerged, then fell back again. I heard a crack, and then a grunt, and then, as though by bitter poets, a cry of hurt and rage. To know what was what or who who was hard, but soon the man rose in deep silhouette, the hatchet aimed at Basil's neck, his face the print of terror.

I rushed in now, my little knife lost, and took the man by his wrist. Straddling Basil, still pinned, he swiveled round to meet me. Those pale eyes—that silver beard and earwig mouth—the hand with the hatchet bony and wet—the tattoos on the fingers—

"*You*," I said.

"No, no," Super said. "Not me." He still had my friend by the throat. Basil tried to speak, but couldn't so much as squeal. "You ain't no bard," Super told him. "Rest a while, now."

"It was you in the basement," I said.

"*We* weren't nowhere near the basement."

"You would've killed him."

The old man snorted. "This little squirrel? Heh. We were just scratching his mortality some. Catch our drift?"

I looked at the hatchet. I looked at Basil. I looked at the hatchet, and then again at this spooky man. And then once more I saw the rain, veiling with its ceaselessness stage and play alike, and knew I was just a groundling.

"I don't suppose you have any more of that stuff," I said, hoping Super would know my intent.

With two fingers he picked a blob of mud from his face and studied it like he might a gem. Then he balled up the blob and squashed it. Next to him, as if he'd been there always, sat Fortinbras the dog.

"Laddie," the old man said, "your telephone has gone kapooey."

"What?" I said.

"But fear not, fear not. The man we used to be just did a bit of surgery. The wires are fine, we think."

"Who is this guy?" Basil said, and I just about laughed. With his blackface of mud he looked a wretched minstrel.

"The one we told you about."

"This crusty boob?"

Super stood quietly by, a quasi-grin working beneath his beard. He'd just topped Basil at his own game, *mano a mano*. But worse than that, he'd shamed him. Looks made Super the grizzled old man half Basil's size. And yet here he was carrying on like the matter had been less than a drill in humor. He could've been the high school jock laying a yo-yo on a freshman nerd.

"*Naw*," Super said. "Don't say it's so."

"You want to cut my throat, dickwad, get on with it. Otherwise, blow me."

"Tell us, Laertes. Just how is it you expect to get our cousin down the mountain?"

"You have any idea what he's talking about?" Basil asked.

I shook my head.

"Stuyvesant Wainwright the Fourth, of course. We come to see that old black clown doesn't carry him off."

"Let's get out of this rain," I said.

"Not till you officiate some manners-making, you won't." I looked at the old man. "Your cohort," he said. "We don't know him from Hill."

Goddamn. Crazy as it was, the geeze wanted introductions. "Super," I said, "meet Basil. Basil, Super."

Super extended a hand. "Pleased to rub truth with you, son."

"Basil. My name is Basil."

The old man scratched his beard. "If we can recollect better than piss in a pot, memory says the name ain't never the thing. Fools of nature's all we are, to the last of us."

Basil turned to me, defeated. "I'm really cold," he said, almost whispering. "And this guy makes me feel like a mollusk. You mind if I kind of just, you know, go inside?"

I ASKED SUPER IN, BUT HE LEANED AGAINST A boulder and pulled off a boot.

"Something," he said, "is itching at us."

Where a foot and five toes should've been was a chunk of salmon-colored plastic. He peered into the boot, tapped its sole, turned it down, and shook it.

"Ha!" he shouted. "Someone needs to ring them bells!"

It was hard to believe, but before my eyes, on the old man's palm, lay a little stone. He examined it, grinning, then looked up like I were a man imprisoned.

"Take this," he said, hand held out, "and we will set you free."

"Don't you ever get cold?"

"We wanted to make sure you got help for Stuyvey. Some investigation after we dropped off you and him revealed that a sore impossibility, hence our return. We are good with wires."

Again I made away but the old man wouldn't budge. A pallor had crept over him now, a rich air of sadness.

"Not that we'd recommend such activity beyond the pure necessities," he said, and turned toward the light someone in the cabin had just switched on, "given our mission's success and your telephone does now work."

Dinky and Hickory were gazing down from one window, Lucille from another.

"So how'd you know about that thing anyhow?" I said, indicating the little stone.

"Ever hear that old saw," he said, "'All the world's in a grain of sand?'"

"If I did, I don't remember."

Super tossed the stone and donned his boot. The last thing he wanted, it seemed, was to go inside. I recalled his truck's open windows, his refusal of Dinky's invite. Finally he stood and called his dog Fortinbras, then cleared his throat for speech.

"After the doctors pitched them boys in the Cong the better half of our two legs," he said, "—hold on now, let us ponder… that was back in March of '68, we believe, Tet offensive is when the foul deed done been done—well, like we said, after they snatched it off the way they did and throwed it to the dogs what with only a scratch, we didn't have any more sense where it had been than a germ has brains. But later we got to feeling these itches down there, and other pains and whatnots. Our ghost foot, they called it. We can feel, all right."

After that, what I really had to say couldn't be said. I was just too tired.

"You're welcome to come inside," I said. "But whatever you do, I've got to go."

"Well you go on and go, then, though again we must decline. We only hope you and yours got enough of that blister-your-sister up there to last the night or more. In case nobody told you, there's a bastard of a flood in progress as we speak. The spirits are truly calling."

A CIRCUS-MUSIC AIR SEEPED THROUGH THE WALLS, a voice croaking on about whispers and dances and the lie that was home. It was the mongoloid glee of pots and pans, and marimbas, and accordions, and guitars that wouldn't tune. And like the song, all inside was doorway huddlings and splashing wine, the mirth, it's true, of fantastic ends. The world had changed between now and then, but the cabin had not, nor the humans in it. How is it the strangest people we know are nearly always ourselves?

My boys and girls were at it again, none of them eager, of course, to know how we'd fared. The two girls and Dinky sat round Basil sprawled on the floor with a bottle in his fist.

Lucille was making a pile from the mud she'd pinched off her man. She paused when I walked in, more, it seemed, from the disturbance I'd created than anything else.

Dinky had propped himself on an elbow to motion at his drink. No doubt he'd struck the pose merely to impress. In all our years, our lasting pride was standing off the Comedown.

The Comedown—ah—what's got to be the nearest drunks can get to Old Scratch's terror when Sir Nothing cast him out—far from your mother's kisses and the SweeTarts bought on Sunday with the coins from Saturday's chores after waffles and bacon and eggs—crushed in that void, totally confounded: Jim

Carroll's lovely at the corner of Seamen and Dripp, who every Friday night bangs this jerk or that to rise come *mañana* with a frog in her throat and Ding Dongs and beer and rubs on the floor: the tone arm's bouncing in "Angie's" last groove, the stench is sick as a cheeseburger's ghost, the light through the blinds are the fires of hell, and *nothing*—nothing like a blot—of true love is lost in the depths of her hair. Still, and for all that, you'd never find us giving in to the thing, admitting our defeat, not ever. The Comedown could gouge our eyes and break our teeth, stab us and choke us and carve its name in our heads, but we'd only scream for more. It didn't matter that we'd slipped down its throat, our hands gone utterly wild. Fuck that beast! It could swallow us whole! And whenever we did find ourselves in that dark fix, really and truly—and we did, we did—you'd not once hear us say it. Someone came along to ask our thoughts, they'd get the old two thumbs. Serve up that grime. Serve up the shit entire. We'd be there sure with bibs besides, slurping it down to the drop.

Something good and mean had Dinky all right, if not the Comedown then some other such piece of woe. Anyone could see it. He gazed out emptily now, frogish and huge. A person could've slapped his face with a skunk or crammed his ass full of melon, he wouldn't have squawked a peep. His face didn't lie. It was a fallen house, in whose halls slunk that oaf, Remembrance.

"You're back," he said, struggling to his hands and knees. He couldn't decide to stay put or stand, or even what to say. "Welcome once again, old pal… to our little… fold."

And then Hickory rose to greet me, the shag fell away, goofy and light she floated my way, petals in her hair and from her eyes, though still I was numb, still my head was a bucket of sand, that floating blossom, dancing girl, she came my way to pour herself out and smother me gold, it was only for me to cry the word, her with her voice, her with her lips and eyes, for now I was home, made limber and fine, another time yet I'd been brought clear, I could smell her now, she drove me bent, hallelujah, lord, praise be the stars, for man, oh man, this I knew, I was most certainly fucked…

"Look at you," she said. "Your face…"

They were gawking at me, then, all of them, the mannequin, too, staring me down with its empty eyes. Then clarity took me, and I snatched up the mannequin to kiss it again and again. And then I tucked it in my arm and with my free hand high went forth.

"My friends!" I said. "My friends!" I grabbed a bottle and poured five shots. "I'd like to propose a toast!"

"Come again?" Lucille said.

"A toast, my dear. In fact, a toast to you. In honor of your promotion." I raised my glass. The spirit of the underground man had crept into my head, through the porch of my sleeping ear. "Let us all drink," I shouted, "to the success of Lucille Bonnery. May she live long and prosper in her new status as Queen of the Corporate Raiders!"

Dinky found the strength to burble "Hear! Hear!" while Basil sat up with "I'll drink to that—hell, I'll drink to anything!" They emptied their glasses with a single draught, Hickory and Lucille, too. "A toast!" they said, and drank.

I choked down my shot and began to convulse…

When at last I came to from an apparent fit of speaking in tongues, Basil was standing above me, rubbing his eyes. He looked hideous and comical, encrusted with mud, it and that hat perched on his head like some ugly bird from the sea.

"Maybe you guys've got the skinny from the inside," he said, "but I haven't understood half the crap this whacko said."

"So your question is…?" Lucille said.

"*Hatchet Lady!*" Hickory said.

"Nice," Dinky said.

On the mantle, between a badly carved falcon and some frou-frou matches, stood a little doll from Mexico, huaraches, serape, sombrero, all. When you pulled the sombrero off its head, a giant boner sprang from its pants, only some wise guy had wedged a twig beneath the thing's sombrero to keep the boner boned.

I held up the mannequin like some ventriloquist's dummy. "This is not a prison," it said. "Because if it is, what the heck is the world?"

Dinky coughed. "Well put, mannequin," he said.

"You, my fat-headed friend," said Basil as he whirled on Dinky with more savagery than he seemed able, "had better watch it."

Dinky fell into another fit, his worst so far. Super had returned to fix the phone, I remembered. That's what he'd been doing in the basement, working on the wires for the phone. If the phone worked, we could call for help, we could bring in a winch for Basil's truck. And if the roads hadn't been washed away like They were saying they might, we could run our friend to the doc's and throw a celebration. And if the phone didn't work, well, Super had got here somehow. If he was here, so was his truck.

Fancy ideas, and probable, too, had the phone not been made worthless for good. From the other room, the news warned folks trapped in the storm to remain inside with patience. Mr and Mrs Jones would love this, I thought, free of the flood in their cozy dens. They'd hunker round the tube with their top-shelf booze and gourmet ale to point and exclaim, taken for a time from gluing their models or paging through zines or waking from another nap.

Dinky was hacking so bad my friends couldn't help but see. They gathered round him now, outrageous. They wouldn't admit it, not yet, but the sons of bitches were scared. Dinky looked worse than he had in the rain. "What's wrong, what's wrong?" Hickory said, and cried.

Pretty soon they got him on the couch, and pretty soon again he set into the lines from some old poem while making gestures no one could stop. "Dinky's sick," he said. "He must die—Lord, have mercy on us!" Then he'd cough or burble or whimper or sometimes even laugh. And then the tedium would repeat.

"That's not funny, Dink," Basil kept saying. "That's not funny."

"It's no joke," I said.

"Really?" Lucille said. "Maybe you could tell me what you're doing with that mannequin then."

"Not right now," Basil told her. "Just don't."

"Well," Lucille said, "then maybe *you'll* let me know when I've got your permission, O Lord of Lords."

"I'm serious, Lucille."

I dropped the mannequin and kicked it. "Now you're serious. It takes Stuyvesant getting like this for you to get serious."

"That supposed to mean something?"

"Unbelievable," I said.

"What, like you've been telling me something?" Basil said. He flung his hand toward Dinky. "I mean, look at the bastard."

Hickory's face had become a mask, not so much of sadness or despair, though these were plain, too, in a tired sort of way, but more of simple disgust. "Someone get me a towel," she said. "And another pillow."

We heard Lucille in the kitchen rifling through cupboards and drawers. From another room a door skreeked open, and Lucille returned with a rag and icky pillow.

"The situation's evident," I said. "But if we stay here much longer we might not be able to leave."

"Anyone can see he's sick, *dork*," Basil said. "A fucking bat in a goddamned fucking cave could see that."

"*Dinky's sick, he must die—Lord, have mercy on us!*"

Hickory took the rag from the bowl and passed it over Dinky's head. She caressed him with easy words.

"Anyone," I said, "could've seen the guy was sick a-way back when, *squeeze*. But no one here gave a goddamn till the shit was in their face."

"Who cares?" Lucille said. "The point is we give a damn now. At least I do." She looked like she'd just been indicted for some heinous crime. Her eyes leapt from face to face. "I *do* care," she said.

"Not enough," I said, "to've ever been straight with him. Not when you had the chance."

"I know you're not talking about what I think you're talking about."

"Just how many were there before the Gladden brothers, Lucy? How many after?"

"That's not fair, AJ."

"Or what about telling us all why you didn't care for Dinky enough to confess the fun you were having that summer he was away? Or any other time you couldn't shrug off your seven-month itch."

I was getting to her all right. She was crumbling. "That's not fair," she said.

"You think he doesn't know all about your games?"

"*You* don't know the half of it, you bastard," she said. "I had my reasons."

"You did," I said. "And I know the hole they crawled out of."

"That's not fair. It's not fair."

"It's a little hard to cry wolf when you're one of them."

"None of that stuff had anything to do with how I feel about Dinky. How would you know what he means to me?"

"I wouldn't, Lucy. That's my point. I can't see you give a stinking straw for the son of a bitch."

"You bastard."

I ignored her and went on. "Is that what you told Basil last summer, fucking him under that Mexican moon? I know how you are, Lucy. Hang the cost! *Shit.* You care so much for Dinky you just sent him into a hurricane for a bag of ice."

Basil rose. "I should cave your skull in right fucking now."

My hands flipped up to frame my face with a set of waggling fingers. Somewhere in my heart I'd hoped to look like Munch's screaming man. "I'm sooooo fwightened," I said. And then I snarled. "You cock head. If you had anything in your skull to make it worthwhile, I'd have done you a lifetime back."

Basil stood there in his suit of mud. He still had that blackface, and the hat besides, perched on his head like an ugly bird.

"I'm your *boss,*" he said. "Remember that? In fact, now that I think about it, I'm your *former* boss."

"I never worked for you."

"I suppose I'm not the one who's been signing your checks these last eight years then."

"You jerk. Everyone here knows your grandma owns the buildings. That she got from your grandpa no less. All of which makes you nothing but a trust-fund piece of crap with insurance and fancy clothes."

My friend was fazed, I could see, but that didn't keep him from shooting back. "It's a hell of a lot better than being a talent-lacking toilet-scrubber," he said.

"*Dinky's sick, he must die—Lord, have mercy on us!*"

Hickory had stayed by Dinky throughout, hand-in-hand,

passing the rag along his brow. Now she turned our way with liquid eyes.

"Please, you guys," she said. "Stop."

"*Dinky's sick, he must die—*"

"Shut up!" Basil said.

"Dinky," Lucille said, "we're going to get you out of here."

"After Pac Bell comes in to fix the phone we might," I said.

"*Dinky's sick, he must—*"

"Dinky," Lucille said.

"*He must die—Lord, have mercy on us!*"

"He doesn't even know what he's saying anymore," Hickory said.

"Maybe Super's still around," I said.

"What?" said Lucille.

"*Fuck* that guy," said Basil.

"No," I said. "I mean, if he's around, so's his truck. He had to get here somehow, didn't he?"

"*If* we can find him," Hickory said.

"Maybe we can. Me and Basil, I mean. At least we can try."

"The hell *I* am. After what he did to me?"

"What *he* did to *you*?" said Lucille. "I thought you said he was just some old nut."

"But you don't know. The guy's a freak, as in for real. It's like he's the actual *devil* or something."

"That doesn't mean he won't help us," I said.

"I'm not going anywhere."

Another fit had settled over Dinky, the coughing again, the same spewing again of blood and phlegm. I smoothed his blanket and dabbed his mouth. Hickory told me to kill my smoke, so I got up and took about fourteen slugs of bourbon. Then I went into the storm, hollering out for some wild old man, with his wasted monkey and bed of dolls and dog standing quietly by.

An emptiness had opened up inside me. The night was wet and black and empty and cold, and I was scared, more so than I'd ever been. Maybe this is *it*, I thought, maybe this is where I'll see the face no one but the dead have ever seen. But maybe I won't be dead, just almost-dead, just passed out kind of in a forest of mud, curled up like some little bald worm in the mud.

THERE ARE TIMES YOU SEE THE ROT YOU'VE always been. My days were a trail of liquor-store bumblings and sunrise guilt, and every penny I'd earned these years had come to rest in a dirty glass. I'd ceased caring for others, and definitely for myself. The only things that mattered were booze and books. Scrubbing toilets—the very ones I'd puked into so many times—that was what I knew. The hurly burly of solitude that took me come each day's midnight had stripped any cool I might still have owned a long time back. Night after night, in the chill of an empty school, my ambitions fell away like leaves from boughs in autumn. And wandering those halls, moving from bin to toilet to bin, the few kind trophies of memory that did remain floated by as evil nymphs—evil because angelic, angelic because there in the corridors of my past those trophies were safe from deeper ruin. And like angels they were accessible in only the cruelest of ways. What was the good in having something you could never hold?

Dozing behind the desks in that collegiate gloom, the times of my youth would tiptoe up with a sort of wary glee, now days of drowsing in my grandfather's swing, now lightning in a field. Grape juice popsicles melted in my hand, beneath the shade of a swaying oak. My young mother would come to play in the wading pool. And rustling leaves, and tinkling ice, and the buzzing of bees, and pie…

And now? Now I was a shrunken head…

In the cabin some jazzy swing had commenced. Any other day it would've been a finger-snapping bop for Lucky Strikes and gimlets and velvet gowns on creamy skin, spiffed up wing-tips and watches on fobs, dipping your darling with her mouth full of giggles and hot white teeth—Bobby Darin crooning for the sharks and the billowing blood. But that was not the case tonight. Tonight was a heckler in the dark.

I remembered in the midst of my shouting the light I'd seen through the trees when after the wreck Super brought us home. Dinky had said he had no neighbors, but if that were true, what was behind the light? A couple hundred yards down the road, I met another that spliced away, made just of dirt albeit. At first I couldn't see zilch, much less a would-be light. The wind roaring as it was, the water coming down as it was, not from the sky at the moment, but from the trees, with needles and leaves and dirt, and the groaning of the trees and rush off the mountain of water still in sheets, it was all I could do to keep from turning back. It seemed to me the notion of a boob to walk up that road alone—surely I'd deserve whatever I got. Who knew what I'd find, if not Super or a neighbor then may chance a pissed off lion, as scared as I was scared and hungry as hell besides. And what if I did find a man, but that man was no neighbor or even a neighborly man, but the kind Basil had always feared, the freak in the plastic suit, with six fingers and toes and a penis on his chin, wielding a flamethrower and Sawzall both? Not good, not good, any way you sliced it, not a bit of it was good. On the other hand, who the frick cared what I found? If I did nothing, chances we all croaked up here on the mountain wouldn't be so slim. Certainly Dinky wasn't going to mend. The guy needed a doctor, pronto. Not to mention if I ran off now, down the line I'd have to live with myself, a prospect at its best unspeakably vile. Getting killed was preferable to such a fate, honestly. I hoofed it up the road therefore on a bit less than faith, my adrenalin pumping as I stumbled along. And then I saw it, like before, a single light shining faintly through the trees. So it was actually there. So I had not been totally tripping. And lights meant power, and power, human beings. My eyes swelled bigger, then, I was ready for the worst, though just what I'd do when the worst came down, the best could never say. The road wound toward the light, but dwindled soon to a shabby trail leading higher up the mountain than the light had had me guess. Oh well. I'd gone this far, and now I had to see it through. The trail wended on, this way and that, until abruptly it debouched onto a tiny glade crepuscular with the light of a bulb on a wire through trees about twenty feet up. In the middle of the glade was a grimy tent, that was all, shaking in the wind. I cast about, struggling to discern a figure or shape, something squirming hogtied in a bag near the edge of the glade, I didn't care, I only wanted the what-was-what, even if that what was drastic. But I saw nothing but the rickety tent—not a clothesline, not a fire pit, not a chair or box or ice chest or stove, just a rickety, grimy tent. It simply didn't make sense, this scene. What was the source of this odd light's power? And who needed light to sleep in a tent, since pretty plainly nothing else was happening here? And why even a tent, in this of all wicked places? The last thing I wanted was to look inside, but knew I couldn't do other. That no doubt would be the test. The tent could even have been booby trapped, I thought. The freak with his bear-hide cowl and dick-chin and bones could be lurking anywhere, really, patiently waiting me out, itsy bitsy fly that I'd then be. And that was all it would take, my stepping into the creepy glade, whereon the fiend could drill an arrow through my neck or maybe just wait snaggletoothed and grinning till I stepped in the jaws of the trap he'd camo'd at the front of the tent, then rush up to hack out the pieces of me he'd forthwith set to slobbering on while writhing in eldritch pain and eldritch horror I lay by watching, pathetic. A few minutes of this whimsy later, having been struck that I could stand there forever conjuring the scene of my demise, I set toward the tent, listening through the wrack for some atypical sound, however teensy, however bright, anything to presage if only by an instant my impending harm, pressing on through the aura the hammer of my heart had generated round me, turned by now half-puke/half-stone, my legs prehistoric sarcophagi. My vision had contracted into the space of the tent itself, buffered all around by a band of quivering mist. And the closer I drew, the farther away the tent seemed to get, until in the space of a step the distance vanished, and there I stood before the tent. It seemed almost a being itself, the tent, its canvas in the wind like the skin of a creature from the sea or the north, a leviathan, suddenly, hunkered in the mud, I could easily have believed. Somehow I'd taken the zipper in hand, itself already half undone, and slid it till the entrance material had crumpled at my feet. And yet when I leaned into the tent, expecting who knows what to materialize before me—a stack of corpses, a cache of grub, magazines of ammo, maybe, tent-top high—what should I find but… nothing. The tent was as empty as a dead man's mind, not a scrap to be found, nothing so much as a wayward battery or dented cup, nor candy bar wrapper nor length of string nor nubbins of some candle. And it was then I saw the nature of terror, because it was then the nature of my predicament, like a toxic cloud, swallowed me utterly up. Terror, I realized, had nothing to do with time and space but with the absence of them, and with the incomprehensibility of that absence. There before that rotting little tent empty in the night in the glade in the forest in the heart of a pulsing storm, the emptiness of my life, and of my aloneness in it, usurped my thoughts with cruelty I couldn't fathom. A cipher just the moment before, the tent was now clothed in the powers of a totem, implausibly vicious, and I was numb head to toe, not a single atom free. I turned away in my deadness and broke through the night, blind, numb, thoughtless, empty, dead, Frodo in his fog of malice having donned that hideous Ring. I don't know how long I ran, but only that I ran till the earth resolved to steal my feet. My face had hit the mud at the base of the trail. I'd tripped on a branch, and lay in the mud, now, gasping for breath as once again the rain came down. When finally I rolled over and planted my hand, instead of the sense of slimy mud, the crinkle of cellophane brought me to. And what should that cellophane be part of, I saw, but an empty pack of smokes, Pall Malls, no doubt, goddamn. I dropped the thing and ran up the road shouting once more for Super. I shouted and cried, but come the fork at the road to the cabin, I'd seen nothing, Super most of all. What was the use. There was no use. Nothing mattered. Uselessness ruled. The numbness had left me. *I* had returned, my body in woe, the wet and the cold and the bitterness of my presence in their midst. I put my hands in my pockets and chin on my chest and stumbled toward the cabin.

It wasn't long before, unbelievably, he reappeared, that weird old man, hobbling up from a path to the lake, Fortinbras at his heel. My heart at first leapt with fright—after all I'd been through, my expectations lapsed, I no more thought I'd see him again than a witch. But there he came, lurching along with his earwig mouth, and I knew it would help little to speak of the tent and certainly of where he'd been. Super hadn't been merely *out there*, but *out there and everywhere else.* He *liked* it out there. *Out there* was where the bastard *lived.*

"We hadn't planned on leaving you down and friendless, young Horatio," he said, "if that's what brings you through this rage."

"Dinky needs help, right now," I said, shivering, "but the phone's still dead."

"You know like we know that the closest you are to another phone is a generous league. You seen the distance between here and the next abode."

I put a hand on his shoulder. Like his hands, it felt hard as ivory, and cold. Even out here I could smell him—cigarettes, marijuana, blood. "But what about your place?" I said, desperate, knowing as I spoke the vanity of my words. "Don't you live somewhere here nearby? Don't you have a phone?"

"Your phone, boy, was fixed and fixed. If it don't work, nobody's does." He may as well have handed me a rock. "Where's Laertes?" he said. "We'll be needing his size for the expedition we have in mind."

"He's a little scared of you," I said.

"And yet what with our wheels knee high in mud, we require a beast of his mass."

Super's company back to the cabin was welcomer to me than his presence was to Basil at it.

"Is he kidding?" he said when I told him Super wanted his help.

The old man stood just outside, smoking and sucking his teeth. "Come with us, now, Laertes," he said, and leaned in and pointed at Dinky. "Any little fuzznuts can see what our good cousin's worth. And as for young Horatio here, even if he does have a furious heart, well, he's just a bit too scrawny."

"If you think for even two seconds I'm going out there," Basil said, "into *that*, with *you* no less, you're one hell of a lot crazier than I thought."

Hickory squared herself to Basil. She whispered. "Dinky is sick, Basil. Do you understand?"

"I know it."

"So then pull on your boots and all that and help the man get help."

"How do I know he's not going to slice my throat once he's got me hunched over out there in Shitholeville?"

"You should be ashamed of yourself."

"If he was going to mess you up," I said, "he'd have already done it."

"That's a joke," Lucille said.

"Andrew's right," Hickory said. "Why else would he be here?"

"Oh Laeeeeee-er-teeeees," Super said, sounding like Bugs-Freaking-Bunny taunting Elmer Fudd. Basil said nothing and glared. Super waved his pipe. "We've got a little something for the road, if you catch our drift."

He'd poked my friend where he was soft. Basil knew about Super's drugs. That's a thing he'd never forget.

"And this is no ordinary bud we're talking about," I said. "You get some of what he's got and you'll be riding a freaking dragon."

Basil looked at me and Super and then at Super's pipe. Then he pulled his porkpie down and said, "What's a little more rain?"

DINKY'S HEAD ALONE DIDN'T WEIGH TWO-FORTY. And he wasn't fat, either, just thick as a Nordic killer. And something else that confounded the world, myself included, was his skin, tan all year and, like a doll's, seamless. It was his skin, I figured, that kept folks from seeing what a speed buster he'd been those years at Hastings, when the professor would call him out to say, for instance, whether a man who'd signed a contract with another man and then stabbed that man with a pencil could be held liable, given he'd met his contractual obligation—*Mr Wainwright, will you please explain?*—and Dinky, insomniacal, garbed rain or shine in rugby shirt and Bermuda shorts, would totter from his seat to hold forth like a limey MP. But just as the class thought itself with a kook, Dinky would somehow manage to conjure the magic words. "And finally, sir," he said that time I accompanied him, "since the injury in question has nothing to do with said contract, it should rightly be considered a circumstance actionable in tort. Thus, by virtue of precedent, that being Tabucchi vs. Collins, 1976, the answer to your question must be indisputably affirmative." And that was him. He'd huff and he'd puff like some crook on the lamb, but unless he wanted you to see it, what you saw was a man turned gold from days on a lounge in the sun, impeccable coif and skin.

Well, he was huffing and puffing now, only his hair was gone and his skin like a plum in dirt. He was so far out, in fact, it took us all to drag him to his room. We got him in the bed with his snot rags and porns, and when the gang withdrew, Basil grumbling about the dope Super'd best give him, Dinky and I were left with no one for comfort but the clown on the wall, chained to its horrible stasis.

Super as it happens never did give Basil the pipe. Fiend that he was, the old man tormented my pal, dangling the pipe before him like some thingamajig of beckoning. He knew full well Basil couldn't resist trying to snatch it. The two slogged along for what Basil later described as "a shitload of time," up the road opposite their aim, until at last they wound about headed toward the 50, by which time Basil had been reduced to beggary, and then to outright theft. Predictably, he said, he waited till Super lost himself in a rant on the treachery of winter before lunging at his pocket. Super, however, unlike Basil, wasn't born at night or a fool. In short order, he slammed my friend against a tree and stuck a cutter to his throat while Fortinbras locked fangs on his ankle. Basil just stood there—what else?—helpless before the pictures in his mind, he said, though in the end they surrendered to a single image—Gomer Pyle's face, grinning like the village dolt. *Surprise! Surprise! Surprise!*

For a long time I didn't know a thing about this tale. Had Basil not called me a few months later, after I'd moved away and rented a shack by the river in Portland, I wouldn't have known anything but what he'd told me the first time round, all of which, as it turns out, was a lie. But he did tell me, and, for what it was worth at the time, given our fix, I believed him.

The way he put it, Super slammed him against that tree strictly to air the knowledge he'd got these years wandering the vasty planet. There Basil stood, looking into Super's eyes, knowing that for the second time in his life he was crippled. Oddly,

Basil said, he almost enjoyed that sensation of helplessness, the compulsion, he said, actually to submit. I said *You're joking* and he said *No* and I said *So then now you're addicted to crack?* and he said *I'm telling you, it just happened*, and that was that, he went on to lay it down.

No one had witnessed his fall, he said, but Super and his dog. And if no one had seen it, how could they use it against him—at some later date, he meant, to fuck with him at the Roxy for instance or maybe the Coconut Teaszer, as he hooked into some under-aged nubile with bocci-ball tits and the ass of a little boy? He found it damn near relaxing to let Super rant on with his deep, rumbling voice. It sounded like music, almost, cozily uncertain, uncertainly familiar. Whenever I tried to butt in, Basil got all Zen and proceeded with the sappy, parson-like tongue he invoked most times for dramalogues. What with Super's voice, he said, and the rain thrumming down and the wind through the trees, the moment made him think of some New Age soundtrack these sandal-wearing meat-haters use to fall asleep when they traipse into town. He even went so far as to confess he couldn't tell whether he loved the old man or hated him. He wavered between wishing he could stay there forever, he said, cradled in Super's zany wisdom, or hoping someone might come along with a pistol to pop a cap in the old man's ass.

It grieved him to his heart, Super said, that the powers had ever made human beings, and worse, that he'd been born unto them. He praised the storm if only that it might blot from the earth not just him and Basil but all humankind, people together with animals and creeping things and creatures of the air. The earth was corrupt, he said, the earth was filled with violence.

But each time Basil tried to leaven Super's weight, he gave him a taste of the cutter, and a squirt of fetid breath would escape his teeth, and his eyes would roll up, and he'd set again to ranting.

He swore about certain pods of anguish, of how soon, on a bed of niggardly hearts and jealous bones, beaks sewn shut with thread and the toes of babes hacked off with shears, those pods would blossom into flowers of spleen, and the colossus of venality humanity had become would shudder and by crappers crumble in that swarm. Super was mad. The moon had come too near, he said. The eagle should never have landed. And the man on the moon was a whoreson goon and all the world his toilet. Basil looked skyward, and by godfrey there it hung, the moon, peering through the clouds like the eye of a giant owl. Even as they spoke, Super told him, they were bound by a Gordian knot and that, *ecce signum*, here be the storm that corresponded to the storm in the eye of another storm yet, turning on itself and turning on its turn.

"We're just varlets in a void," Super said, Basil said. "The stratosphere was a lovely basket before the likes of you and me and the man we used to be come along with our fubbings and shoggings and horses from the same bleeding opera evening after absurd evening. Don't you know, boy? Don't you know?"

Basil stayed pressed to the tree, silent and amazed, feeling he should know, feeling he *did* know, but for all his trying couldn't say. And even if he could've said it, he wouldn't have. Because he wanted the old man to say it for him. At that moment, Basil felt as if Super's words somehow possessed the amplitude of prophecy. He could've said *Orangejuice* or *Snot* or *Duran Duran* and Basil would've found some meaning. The geeze had been trying to teach him something, but Basil, insolent and ingrate, had been unwilling to learn. Again he tried opening himself to the old man's hoodoo but felt he was nothing to him but a trinket with which he could entertain himself until ennui sent him forth once more to search. When finally Super had resumed his speech, it seemed to Basil the sun should've risen and the storm passed. But not a minute had passed, much less an hour. The old man's fingers loosened, the cutter fell away. Basil could scarcely blink or breathe, the old man had been squeezing him so. A protracted shiver ran through him as he gazed into Super's face, and then an icy numbness. The old man grinned. The grin became a chortle and the chortle a laugh, an obscenely sinister sound that seemed from the throat of a ghoul. And yet again Super dangled his fancy pipe. "You can't always get what you want, boy," he said. "Just what you need." Then he turned up the road, Fortinbras at his heel.

Basil felt ultimate disappointment. Super had lied. More heinous still, he'd stolen his lie from a song by one of Basil's most idolized bands, those five timeless beings who with sheer cheek and scorn for so-called bourgeoisie protocol had achieved a stature very near to that of God and second only to Iggy Pop, who was himself God (after all, Basil had said on numerous occasions, no one but God could survive on peanuts and bloody marys and bihourly main bangers of the jeweler's little kid, and then hit the road to put on the show Iggy put on night after night, and any dork foolish enough to say otherwise must be summarily flogged). And not only had Super lied—he'd had audacity enough to fob the notion off as his. Now the words would be forever leashed to his condescending growl. Not to mention, again, they were a lie. Basil had always got what he wanted, for as long as he could remember. And yet, he thought, if that were so, why was he standing alone in the dark in a storm?

*You can't always get what you want.*

He'd wanted to shout after Super, to tell him how full of shit he was, that he didn't, as Dinky'd always said, know his ass from fat meat. But Basil only stood there, absurd, swathed with the mud the old man had given him a rolling in. He peered through the gloom, hoping some face from his past might appear, cheesy and smiling, to reassure him—Potsie Weber or Mr Rogers or the Charmin Man—but nothing of the sort. Super had gone for good.

*You can't always get what you want.*

But goddamn it, maybe Super hadn't lied. When Basil looked at his life, he had to confess that nothing he really wanted had fallen his way. He'd wanted, for instance, to be a rock star since that day in '75, when he'd gone to see KISS at the Cow Palace (in the middle of "Rock and Roll All Nite" Paul Stanley had skittered across the stage with his famous mouth and eye, straight toward the hirsute but awestruck teenager, and flung his monogrammed pick right at him; after all these years Basil still carried the thing; he loved it so much, he always bragged, he intended someday to bestow it on his eldest child as a principal family heirloom), and yet They hadn't deemed him worthy. His grandparents by then had of course already given him more money than he could spend, but not a dollar in the pile had lured Fame his way, the old pimp, nor the love and attention he'd thought Fame would bear.

But more than the rest, Basil longed for a father, or for the return of the father he'd had. Come Basil's seventh b-day the swindler told the boy's mother he needed to run an errand. On his way back, he promised, he'd nab some Otter Pops and Fritos for the imminent bash. Instead the villain bailed—caught a number 15 AC Transit to the Fruitvale BART, a train to Civic Center Frisco, a jitney to SFO, and thence a plane to Puerto Vallarta, where he rendezvoused with a recently immigrated Hungarian secretary from the accounts department of Kilpatrick Baking Company, Oakland, California, a woman whom only three months earlier he'd bought a new nose, two grand. The mula for this he'd conned from another mark yet, a senior citizen named Mrs Annabelle Lovejoy, exstripper, pornstar, and erstwhile mentor to Bettie Page—yes, *the* Bettie Page—who, Mrs Lovejoy, had been making regular monthly deposits of 500 smackaroonies into Basil's father's account, under the presumption, as the tale gets told, that he in turn would soon begin work on a private ranch in southern Nevada, a discreet, albeit fully indulgent, men's club. And once bolted, Basil's father never returned. Nor did he so much as call, nor even send a card. His mother learned of his father's whereabouts four years later, by happenstance, from a grocery clerk at Lucky's whose husband knew a bookie Basil's father was up to his neck in debt to. He'd left his Hungarian nosejob for the daughter of a snake-charming preacher from the Church of the Redemption of the Lost Apostles, Woodland, CA. Yes, he'd got religion now, and in the biggest way. Holy-rolling via cable from his own late-night soap box (much like the infamous Dr Scott), he and his sermons (authorized of course not only by the good Lord Himself but as well by a PhD from Dr Ronald Hassler's Night School for the Ecclesiastical Faithful, Soledad, CA, just a block down the street from the prison) could now be seen and heard in more than fifty-five municipalities throughout the Great Central Valley. Not until Super had appeared, Basil said, had he admitted how very much he'd missed his father, and yearned for his father, and for his father's love. He'd wanted his father's love for as long as he could remember, really, badly enough that ultimately that wanting had parleyed to a hurt only a bottle or bud or rock could ease. They, however, hadn't seen fit to grant him this, either, this revenant daddy.

Basil found himself shortly crying out, and more than once at that, but for answer got only the wind and rain and the creaking of trees in the wind and rain. To the west he could see the void that was the lake, black as the hole of his hurt. Lights winked at its edges, a perforated thread which for now was all that stood twixt the town and its destruction.

Basil began to shiver. At first he managed to contain his fear, but as it all continued to mingle and grow, his loneliness and guilt and disconsolation, so too did its outward display. Something had been taken from him, that much he knew, and yet precisely what he couldn't explain. Or perhaps he was simply lost. He knew only that with the ferocity of some malevolent germ the sense he'd been living a protracted mistake was devouring what little of him remained. And then he wept into oblivion.

When he came to, he said, he was so cold that should someone so much as tap him, his body would shatter like an effigy of ice. But the longer he waited, the more deeply he'd be lost. He didn't have his hatchet. He didn't have even a knife.

And so visions of catastrophe rollicked through his mind. Any minute now a tour-bus jammed with cultic octogenarians might descend on him, strayed from the path to some Lawn Bowling Tournament for Abused Geriatrics. They'd have painted faces and doctor's smocks, wooden dentures and powdered wigs. They'd sport bifocaled pince-nez, diapers by the ream, and with their embroidery needles tipped in poison they'd set to work on his flesh as though a hopelessly imperfect doily. Or maybe something worse, a heretofore undiscovered tiger perchance, the last of its kind pouncing from the dark with nuclear fangs. Or maybe a swarm of winter-loving bugs, clawing through the earth to feed on his brain. But worst of all, he fantasized, much worse, he said—and here, at this possibility, Basil felt what he only later realized was the essence of panic, of real human terror—a colony of Lilliputian Deadheads might emerge from the boroughs of patchouli they'd fashioned in the trees about him, roaring about in a murder of Lilliputian schoolbuses, each painted in patterns of red, white, and blue, replete with toupéed death-heads, all of the groupies with their nasty feet and rastafied haberdashery, macraméd roach clips, earthenware bongs, Moosewood Cookbooks and astrology charts, organic cottonwear, dreadlocks, Greenpeace and tarot cards, too, and the diminutive women with their hairy legs and bushes, and the men with their John Muir beards, they'd all truss him up and cram his gullet with Ben and Jerry's Cherry Garcia while around him, from the multitude of Lilliputian tweeders and woofers they'd have installed on the roofs of their Lilliputian busses, the anthemic "Truckin'" would blare, each and every one of these fiends, man, woman, and Muckluckian brat, flailing about in terpsichorean frenzy, The Wiggly-Womp Dance of the Dead. Basil wanted to run but his feet had sunk to the ankles in sludge. Sad but true, the bastard was stuck.

Directly after our conversation that early April afternoon, I walked into the sun to contemplate whether Basil had found any pleasure in his despair. Because now and then, I've heard it said, it's in despair we find our deepest joy, and more so yet when we see the hopelessness of our state. But who's to say? None of us really knows that much.

That night in the rain nearly four days had passed since Basil had slept. The meth was at best a ghost in his veins, and he'd been heavily drinking. Going underground was not an option. He may've been wretched, but he wasn't a mouse. And yet neither was he any longer the man he'd been, if ever he was that man. He didn't know who he was anymore, or what. He knew only that once upon a time he'd scoffed at the delay of action, because delay implied thought and thought, in short, was for pussies. And this for Basil was so. He'd never measured the cost of his deeds—what might happen should he bash this nose or snap that arm, say, or ingest this drug, or bang that drunken lass. Never once had he agonized before probable litigation, damage to the brain, unwieldy prophylactics. All these things Basil would do in a flash, especially if the man was blocking his yen, or the drug could bring him up or down, or the lass was there for the taking. Because Basil too had adopted The Cry of Twentieth-Century Solipsism, come straight from the mouth of his sometime-significant other. *Hang the cost!* he'd shout, and leap into the fray. Never once, in truth, had Basil considered even the *notion* of consequences, not, at least, insofar as that thinking concerned the philosophies of action and reaction, how in his moments of resolution he, Basil, functioned merely as a catalyst for the further realization of as-yet suppressed events.

And so he was trapped in this limbo of grey. He could stay where he was, he thought, and maybe, though more probably, die—a not unattractive notion on the chance we buddies viewed his death as martyrdom—or chase after Super, or return to the cabin to plan new modes of breaking away. But the deeper his reflection, the greater his fear. He couldn't free his feet, much less reach them to touch. He'd grown too stiff, for that matter, even to touch his knees. That was when the panic engulfed him, he said, that was when he fell. So brightly excruciating was his pain that at first he thought it rapture, though it wasn't, of course, or anything distantly like it. Pain pure and simple had struck him, such terribly horrifically appalling pain that the cry he let out could as easily have been heard as rhapsody than ecumenical howl. He pulled his dogs clear of both boots and mud and curled up like a question mark in tears, wanting nothing then but oblivion, or some place instead with quiet and warmth, and a beautiful girl, and booze…

*BOOZE. BOURBON TEA. GIRLS…*

The girls had gone to make bourbon tea, and Basil had left with Super. The door swung open, the door clunked shut. All lay in silence, they were gone.

But then I heard voices, and then a frisky tune, both jovial and odd, bopping to lyrics odder still.

*When my baby makes love to me*, the woman sang, *it's murder.*

Dinky lay on the bed, mumbling against this scene, which by now had become a cinema of useless torture. Nor could I shake free of his mantra. Like evil vines, it had grown purchase in my head: *Dinky's sick, he must die—Lord, have mercy on us!*

The man didn't even seem real anymore. Or maybe he was realer than I could take. I held his hand. I stroked his head. His face felt clammy and hot. Above us, the clown looked content as a louse on a kid, staring with that sinister smile, its carnation, withered and doomed, the fucking thing. To hear the timpani of his heart I lay my head on Dinky's chest, but in my ears sang scratching claws. If in that moment a single word could've peeled away all the pretense and falsity behind which our lives had till then squirmed, I would've said that word, and said that word, and said that word again.

*When my baby makes love to me, it's murder.*

The night itself had become a lamentation, the dawn, trudging our way, its unshed tear. I wanted so badly to make up for all I'd done and been. But first I had to make myself, whoever that was, happy, whole, something. How I was to accomplish that, though, redeem myself, when that redemption hinged on so many needs, some impossible giving away of self, only doom could say. When my life amounted to a spoil of fits and starts? When I myself was a fake, if that, endlessly tangled in my web of fear?

I dropped into a chair and let it fade…

Down a slope of brush I tumbled, into a wasted canyon. A host of women rose from the banks of some dead river, their hair, like queens', in chignons pierced by sticks. They had elongated waists and statuary thighs, and their faces were veiled as in some ritualized state of mourning. Bangles and bands and bracelets of steel adorned their arms and wrists. I'd never seen something at once so beautiful and inert, postures, it seemed, intended as much to seduce as repel. I was negotiated through these idols like some apathetic hero, never touching them or land. I didn't speak to them, either, nor did I hear them speak. They were cold, these women, queer, and yet somehow I knew they'd gathered to keep me safe. And then a mouth opened up, the canyon was ending, and I hovered at the breach while a woman's voice sounded in my ear, just a word: *Keys…* I was vomited toward a lifeless plain. Among the rubble of some great alluvial fan I lay until with horror I saw that what had looked from above to be a knoll of rock and wood was in truth a mound of bones. I began to laugh. And when my laughter was exhausted, I fell into a swoon…

I rose to a world of verdure and flesh, maidens in a spring. A breeze caressed me. Birds in shadow sang. I was the voyeur in hiding. I smelled the smell of imminent love. They were angels to the last, each with Hickory's eyes, Hickory's nose, Hickory's mouth of red. But soon the green had melted, and I was made a blur. Murder was a sweet and death the moon. Knowledge entered: I had been so blessed…

*Gesundheit!*

Dinky had been sneezing. He lay propped against the wall, Hickory beside him with a mug of steam across whose side were the words, *Don't Worry, Be Happy!* She must've just come in. On the stool to my side sat a mug of my own. My eyes I kept nearly closed.

"The sleep's done you good," Hickory said.

She'd gathered her hair in a bun and stuck it through with a pen. The tattoo of a skeleton key on the back of her neck whispered in my ear. *I don't know where the lock is now. Do you?* Her face was graceful, quietly sad. It darkened for a time, then the corner of her mouth lifted to a faint encouraging smile.

"Drink this," she said.

"What time is it?" Dinky said, and spat into a rag.

"You know I don't own a watch."

"I want to see how long till sunrise."

Hickory shook her head. "The sun will rise, Dinky. You know that." She dabbed at his nose with a tissue. "Drink this."

"It's all bees now," Dinky said.

Hickory paused, as though digging deep for a clever word. She looked sheepish. "The I'll-be-damned kind or the I'll-be-a-son-of-a-guns?"

"In my head I mean."

"Drink."

"I mean it's not fires any more. Just bees."

Hickory drew back the curtain. She leaned into the window till steam fanned out before her. "Pretty soon," she said, "Basil and that old man will be back with the truck."

"I want to ask you a favor."

Her smile was pretense now for sure. And her voice sounded weaker, the skin on her face was tight. Anyone could see she'd grown thin on all the faking.

"Just so long," she said, "as it doesn't involve taking off my clothes."

"Your name. Hickory, I mean. It's not you."

"Someone here's forgetting that someone else made it up."

"I mean, I was wondering, you know, if you'd mind if maybe I called you by your real name."

"I don't care what you call me. You know that, too."

"Mira then. How about I call you Mira."

"Anything you want, Dinky."

After a time my pal sipped from his mug and said, "I saw you dancing. Tonight, when Super brought us back." Hickory smiled. "I told Andrew you moved like smoke."

"Maybe we can go some time," she said. "The five of us together, when we get out of here?"

"Maybe."

"Dinky."

"Leave me alone now. Can you do that for me?"

"You know that's not what you want."

"I'm really, really tired," said Dinky, crying now.

"No, Dinky," she said, "I won't."

THE MUG BESIDE ME SMELLED OF WHISKEY AND something else, some kind of flower, it seemed. White string dangled from its side. Hickory, I figured, had got resourceful. I cleared my throat.

"I made you some tea, too," Hickory said.

"It tastes like ca-ca," Dinky said, so strange, his face still wet with tears.

"That," Hickory said, "was supposed to be a surprise."

I forced a yawn and then a smile, and took the teabag from my mug. On the end of the string was something like a bandage. "What the hell?"

Hickory's mouth was a tight blue heart. "It's my secret brew."

"Jesus," Dinky said.

"If you really want to know," Hickory said, "it comes from a jam jar."

"A jam jar."

"Like the thing that keeps what you put on your toast?"

I looked again at the so-called teabag. "No toast I've ever had."

"Yeah?"

I studied the thing. The image of a jam jar with a big fly's wings bumped through my head. Then I remembered it, that scene from a few years back, with Lucille.

"Is this what I think it is?"

"You can think it's whatever you want, but it came from a jam jar."

"We've been everywhere there is to go," Dinky said, "and everywhere we've been that's called a tampon."

Hickory meanwhile had kept her mouth tight in that little heart. Now she narrowed her eyes.

"Like I said, *it's from a jam jar.*"

So far as I knew, no one had told Hickory the infamous story of Roper and Lucille. She must've just heard it, from Lucille herself, I guessed, probably while they were brewing this toxic grog.

I'd just come in from a long night of raves south of Market. My pal Bruno and I had hooked up with a pal of his, a shrimp of a cat named Andre. The kid was black as a raven, with a hoop through his septum and bleach his fro—a stripe front to back—and an Angel Flight suit, white, propped by a polyester shirt of midnight black, and gold enough round his neck to've drained Fort Knox. He was the slickest dealer I'd ever met.

But before that even, Bruno and I had dropped a few tabs of X and hit the floor to mix it with the ladies. Three spicy Filipinas caught us gawking and slithered over post-haste, wriggles and tits and laughter. We zoomed in on two and left the third to share till someone else appeared. This went on for who-knows-how-long, ten or fifteen, or forty-five or fifty. What I can say for sure is how once Bruno's chick began to outdo mine, I weaseled my way between them. And by God if it wasn't five minutes more that the girl had grown eight arms, a hand on my chest, a hand in my hair, another on my Jean Jeudi.

"Your cock," she said, "I want it so bad in my mouth."

So that's how it was going to play. I'd give the she-devil what she wanted, all right, but first she needed some good old-fashioned romance. We went on with the dancing and kissing, the girl chanting in my ear the whole damned time, great godly filthy things, working herself up, I could see, into a frenzy. It was only after I'd run my hands across her rack a few hundred times that it struck me things were out of joint. Where, for crying out loud, was all the T&A? And then like a nightmare born I realized this goon had no more cleavage than the side of a train. In a panic I ran my fingers through her hair—a freaking wig, no doubt, coarse as a mop. Still, I had to be sure, and the only way to accomplish that was to stroll through the sanctum sanctorum. The X by then had me like a blight. Half of me didn't give a flying rat's ass what this thing was—part man, part woman, a little bit of beast—the other half swam with horror and rage. I spent a few minutes working up my nerve while whatever it was tried to swab my ear clean with its fruity tongue.

"Oh, sugar," it whispered, "I'm so wet down there, so wet for you."

At last my hand found its way into the drop zone, but—aarrrggghhh!—there in the cleft of a tight little buttocks lay a package bigger than my own. It was true, for sunshine's sake, I'd been played like a Mississippi catfish! My furious little fiend had herself a furious little appetite, yes indeed, and time was moving on. For the tiniest instant, I thought, *Hell, maybe I should just go along with this little snowqueen.* After everything else I'd done to get in this spot, it seemed I deserved whatever came my way. And if that weren't a death blow, I looked around to find me ditched by Bruno. I was on the verge of losing my bird when from out of the crowd stepped Alex, my friend from down-unda, purveyor of smart drugs extraordinaire.

"Drinks are on me," I told my little he-she as I rattled my glass of ice.

"Don't go!" it said. "Cammy don't want nothing but you!"

"Worry not, my sweet," I said, sounding like some dickweed Marlow, and bolted.

"You've got to help me," I told Alex.

"Easy now, mate, easy."

The bastard was sporting a boutonniere, of all things, a carnation garishly red. He adjusted this now with stoned aplomb and stepped back to take me in. Between the X and my terror, my peepers had gone Marty Feldman. From every little cranny nodules of color grotesquely pulsed, and the odor of booze, goddamn, the joint was packed with the stuff to the gills, manhattans and martinis and margaritas and woo woos, and wallbangers and grey hounds and midoris and macs—booze and more booze wherever I turned—and the gut-deep bass and calliope of synths, no horn or string could shape such sound, like the syncopated wailings of alien babies and alien dogs, and the cigarettes and cigars, the perfume and dope and hair spray and mints jostled with the stench of so many wet wool coats—well, stab me in my eyes, the works made me zany, I was itches and sweat, a guy built to spill, no shit, and Alex had not a hint or clue. From a fancy silver case dense with glyptics and birds he selected a smoke and tapped it out and lit it. Then he sat there inhaling the thing like a man who loves cheese, very sauve, very dramatic, his watery eyes aglimmer through the fuzz.

"What's the problem, mate?" he said.

"I am in deep doo-doo, man, as in up to my neck."

"You said that."

"I mean *serious*." It took everything I had to keep from looking at Cammy the Man. "This thing," I said. "It's after me."

Alex puffed out a line of smoke-rings and surveyed the room. "I see a lot of blokes doing their best to snare a little piece running round here. Where's these things?"

"It's not a thing, Alex. It's a ghoul."

"Now it's a ghoul."

"No," I said. "Not a ghoul. A dude." Alex kept up with the fancy inhalations and watery stare. "In drag," I said.

"Now we're getting somewhere." This was all so extremely amusing to him, just another whacked-out night in the city.

"Wait a minute," I said. "Don't look now." Cammy had been staring at me, licking her filthy hungry chops as she wriggled and spun. "The tiny thing with the black wig," I said. "With the halter top with sequins?"

"You've got to be kidding," Alex said, his eyes grown noticeably wetter. "If that's a bloke, I am Sherilyn Fenn."

By now my horror had all but caved to anger. I was near ready to slap this guy. "I'm telling you, man," I practically wheezed.

Alex laid his hand on my shoulder and drew me near. "AJ," he said. "What are you on?"

"Nothing," I said, and studied my feet.

"Nothing, eh? How come nothing's never got my orbs looking like a set of mum's best chiner saucers then?"

"Just a little X is all," I said. "Hardly any."

"A bit of the X, he says." At this point the room was whirling. Alex narrowed his eyes. The guy reminded me of James Bond, early Connery even, say from *Dr. No*. "Here's what I'd do if I were you," he said, patronizing as hell. "Go right back over to that little honey and tell her you're in love. Then take her back home and give her a shank on the kitchen table." He put his hands on my shoulders and turned me round. "Look at her," he said. "She's a bloody beauty, mate. Forget you're tripping and step to it."

"That bloody beauty, as you call it," I said, snatching him up by the collar, "has got a cock the size of your kangaroo-spanking arm." Malapropos, *really*, Cammy now decided to shimmy her way over. "Are you going to help me out," I said, "or what?"

"Sure, mate," Alex said, baffled. "Sure."

"I don't care what you say just so long as you say it."

Cammy rubbed my ass. "When you come back, sugar?" she said. "I miss you."

"Cammy. I want you to meet my good friend, Alex."

"He handsome, too," she said.

"Hello, love," Alex said in that exceptionally Aussie way of his. He extended his fancy case but Cammy waved him off. "Listen," Alex said. "Do you think I could keep your beau for just another minute or two? We've been discussing a bit of business here, and we're just about concluded."

"I'm sorry," I said to Cammy. "I almost forgot about that drink."

"No drink," she said. "Just dance." She licked her filthy chops and took my hands, pulling me toward the floor. "Come dance me, sugar. Come."

"Just give me two shakes of the old lamb's tail," I said.

Cammy must've been as high as the rest, else she would've seen me for the fool I was. Her face assumed a corny pout. "You make me so sad," she said.

"I promise you, love," said Alex. "I'll have your chap back in a New York minute." He put his hand on my shoulder and headed toward the bar. "We'll just be right over here," he said, and smiled yellowly. We eased away at a steady pace until Cammy had returned to the floor. Then we broke into a trot.

"The least you could do," Alex said, seeing I'd already forgotten him in my rush toward the exit, "is offer the bloke who saved your arse a drink."

I handed him a fiver. "I don't want to take any chances," I said.

And now the coat check girl was giving me grief. It turns out I'd lost the ticket for my leather.

"Last time I gave a coat back without a ticket," she said, "I nearly got canned."

She had a web of tribal-style ink creeping from beneath the collar of her vintage coat, some Channel cut with a damask print. She worried her hands on the counter before her, smoothing out a piece of invisible cloth.

If I hung around too long, Alex's slippery doings might go to waste. My little fiend could materialize anytime now, *slurp*, *slurp*.

"Maybe I could tell you what it looks like," I said. The girl paged through a magazine. "I can tell you what's in it," I said. "Whatever you want." She kept up with this dumb act until pretty soon a sleek Cleopatra-type gal approached. Of course she had *her* ticket. The check girl disappeared behind a rack and returned a minute later with a leopard fur coat. "Don't you remember me giving it to you?" I said.

"You give me a ticket," she said, "I get your jacket. *Capiche*?"

If the word *capiche* was bad enough from the mouth of a guy, it was ten times worse from the mouth of some poseur of a girl making six bucks an hour. "But what," I said, "if I never find my ticket?"

The girl shrugged. "What if?"

I wanted my coat, but out even more. Cammy hadn't surfaced. I gave the room a final sweep, then checked my pockets. Turns out the fiver I'd slapped on Alex was the last of its kind. All told, I had some matches with a phone-sex girl, a smattering of lint balls, and $2.50 in change, pennies included. That at least would get me a pack of smokes. If nothing else I could hunker down against some warehouse to wait for the return of Bruno and Co.

Gillian the Peachy Puff girl appeared like a nicotine angel. She laid a hand across my wrist as I began to count my change.

"Stop it, AJ," she said. "Before I get embarrassed." I always did like her cutesy hat and those creamy thighs jacked up on stilettos. She handed me a pack of Camel Lights. "It'll be our little secret," she said, and I could've married the girl on the spot.

"I'll tell you all about it over coffee someday," I said.

Her smile hadn't budged. "If it's anything like the rest of your stories, I'll be getting off cheap."

"It's better," I said.

"You watch out," she said.

Sweet, sweet girl! She pecked me on the cheek and wobbled through the crowd. I tore out a smoke and clottered past a couple of bouncers, a gang of jeans-and-leather tough boys, two dykes creaming uglies in the photo booth. Some girl I'd dumped because of her shit-for-breath squealed my way, but I rolled through, faker of oblivion. The doorway was there, the night cheered me on.

Cattycorner from me a Dashiell Hammett lamp sprayed its glow onto the cab beneath it, a Luxor it looked like through rain, beige and purple as it was. Cars and bikes lined both sides of the street, north to south, and yet for the life of me, I couldn't spot a single crummy soul. No way I was going to stand around waiting for Cammy to show her darling face. Fifteen minutes: if Bruno hadn't appeared by then, I'd split like a banana.

The rain came down in mantles. The street looked like a mirror or pool. A line of traffic signals, steadily diminishing, cycled through their colors until far away, ten or twelve blocks, they merged into that familiar anonymity of concrete, wire, and fog. I took a breath and stepped out from my niche. The storm came down, thick with the odors not just of rain on concrete and paint and metal and wood, but of rain on scum, as well, breaking through that crust of dog-day vomit, and piss and poop and oil. A garbage truck drew into a phalanx of dumpsters with its tusk-like prongs. Out near the bay a klaxon lowed. At first it felt good, the cool and the wet. For one slippery moment I seemed to've been blessed with clarity. The world was truly gorgeous! The world had become a special place! But soon I was shivering, and I saw the streets for what they'd been, rows of cars like great sleepy turtles, pigeons huddled along the warehouse sills, all hyper-graffiti and brick. The billboards over the highway, eerie with faces beaming at banks and cars. The strands of mist about them. The endlessly strobing lights.

A white stretch limo inched toward the club. When finally it stopped before me, the last tinted window in a row of tinted windows began to disappear, until Bruno with his chill-blue eyes gazed dopily out.

"Me and Andre," he said, nervously it seemed, for his loss of words at my new look, or for ditching me, I couldn't tell, "were saying how you'd probably busted a nut or two by now."

"Wouldn't you and Andre like to know."

Andre was kicking it regal as a Space Age potentate. A ginormous mirror lay across his lap, covered with a mound of wings. "Hop in, brother," he said, "and spill your woes."

We rolled on down to another club, monotonous and droll. We did this three more times before I had Andre's driver leave me at my flat on Clinton Park. The rain had ceased, the sun plodding up the East Bay clouds.

At that time I was living with Lucille and a dude named Roper, George, that is, a fattish plucker of banjoes who worked in the mailroom for a stock-broking firm up on California Street. First thing he did each night when he got home in his thrift-store suit was change it for his tie-dye and spin some Dead or other such crap, Crosby, Stills, Nash & Young, or Joplin, or maybe even Dylan's whiney ass. But always it was LPs, and that's because Roper, aspiring Luddite that he was, had long ago made a point to boycott advancing tech, CDs, too, no doubt. Lover of bongs packed with green and steins full of lukewarm Guinness, he was, more or less, a grody son of a bitch.

I crept up the stairs and squatted on the throne to empty out my day's worth of living. A rueful song slippery with clarinets and trumpets had seeped in by way of the neighbors. It made me think of *La Dolce Vita*, that scene where Marcello and his old man are sitting drunk with Paparazzo, watching a carpet of balloons follow the clown once he nods their way. The only thing I wanted now was exceeding dreams. But just as I was masking the proof of my deed with a squirt of the trusty freshener, I heard a low giggle, and then a voice in turn. Thinking these to've hatched from the street, I slithered nearer that way and heard them again, a crazy mix of childish giggle and executioner snarl. They, whoever, were in Lucille's room. I stepped softly now, lest the floorboards creak. This guy, whoever, made it *El Numero Cinco* for the girl in two days under a fortnight. I placed my ear to the door.

"Mommy wants Daddy to lick her jam jar," Lucille said. The man's voice grumbled something I couldn't get. "Come on, Daddy," she said, her words both vampy and firm, "lick my jam jar."

"Not this jam jar," said the man.

*Holy holey*, I thought, *it's Roper!* Now I'd never cared what Lucille banged, but this surpassed all bounds. It wasn't so much her shanking eight million dudes that did me in—I'd coped with that plenty—but of her shanking Roper in particular, in secret, no less, after she'd sworn to the world till her face ran blue he was so grotesque she wouldn't kiss him with a taze. The image of Roper's hairy ass jiggling round Lucille, a-pumping and a-groaning like the porker he was, well, it about drove me to the edge.

With my ear to the door, I couldn't help but see the painting

Lucille had hung on the wall beside it. A naked woman lay on a plain, her neck inhumanly bent. And though her face held enough of grief, its grimace revealed some pleasure, too, a thin, canine joy. But it was her eyes that conveyed the bulk of this sense. They'd rolled up in Spartan bliss, half angel, half wolf. Her face, still scarier, showed Lucille's twenty years down the line, the younger in the old, defeated and sad, and the once-full breasts like moribund flowers, and the bulge of stomach, and the veins in the pit behind the knee, and the clefts of her pappy ankles. Roper's voice grumbled on, louder than before.

"Damn it, Lucy, let go of my head."

"Just one tiny lick," Lucille said.

Blankets rustled, springs groaned. "I'll do all kinds of shit," Roper said as Lucille giggled, "but that's not one of them."

"Since when was a big man like you afraid of a little blood?"

"I'm telling you," Roper said. "I don't lick jam jars while the jam's still in them."

Of course the next day I told Basil what I'd heard.

"*Lick my jam jar, Daddy?*" he said. "Are you serious?"

"I just about cried," I said.

When I told Dinky about the incident he took the Blow-Pop from his mouth and whistled. This was before his head had swelled up like a snake-bit horse, back when he still had hair. "Isn't she the rambunctious little harlot," he said.

That night we went to The Trophy Room. Dinky and Basil and I, and two chicks named Tina and Jimmy Sue, had set up camp near the pool table, waiting for Lucille to return with drinks.

"I don't believe you," Jimmy Sue said to Basil. "I know Lucy, and, unfortunately, I know Roper, too. She just wouldn't do it."

"Talk to Mr Jackson," Basil said. "He was there."

"I don't care if you heard it from J. Edgar Hoover. There's no way it's true."

I cast a look round the bunch. "If I told you the shit I know about our friend Miss Bonnery, you'd run to the clinic for a shot in the ass and a couple of cartons of bug juice."

Basil laughed so hard he coughed up his drink, right there on the table. Tina did her damnedest to freak me with her stink eye.

"Wait till Lucy hears this," she said. "She'll claw your fucking eyeballs out."

"She is the Hatchet Lady," Dinky said.

Jimmy Sue tapped the table. "First of all," she said, "Roper looks like Deputy Dog. Second of all, he's a fat greasy pig with a case of dandruff and breath like rotten chicken. I mean, the guy still wears tie-dye."

"That's true," I said, "every bit. But still."

"Still nothing," Tina said.

"I heard what I heard."

"You're disgusting," Jimmy Sue said.

"You think I like it? Cause I don't. I don't like it a bit. In fact, the shit's already a ghost." I expected one of the girls to come back with some lip, but they only sat there huffing on their smokes. "Listen," I said. "Once I had to take a crap in a public restroom, right? I've never done it before in my life, because next to a hippie, public toilets are about the filthiest, most repugnant things I know. And after you hear this little tale, you'll see why. The commode in question happened to be down at the Kabuki. It's Dan Aykroyd and Bill Murray in *Ghostbusters*, fucking up the monster that looks like the Pillsbury Doughboy on PCP. But I have to pinch a loaf so bad I can't sit still. I do my best to stay, the flick is awesome, only to scurry from the scene like a clam. So there I am, doing my thing, praising the gods and their minions for not making me shit the bed—you can ask Basil the details there—when by the TP hanger I see a hole in the wall. And I'm not talking about some pinhole here. This thing was big as a can. But of course that's not all, because inside this hole, like a picture in a goddamned frame, is a little pink cock with a little pink hand just whacking away, going at it like there's no tomorrow."

"Ahhhhhhhhhhhh!!!"

Anytime I ever told this story I got the standard communal howl. The table was absolutely cringing.

"That's right," I said. "How do you think I felt?"

"I would've kicked that guy's ass so bad," Basil said.

"And why is that, *mon frère*?" I said.

"Are you kidding? My space, man, my mind. The little shit, he invaded you. That's how he was getting off. Thinking about you watching him through that hole."

"*Exactly*," I said. "And now I've got this disgusting image in my head. That I'll never, *ever* be rid of. And every time I see a public restroom, that's what I'll see—a little pink hand jerking away at a pink little ugly cock."

"That's all very splendid," Tina said. "But what's it got to do with you lying about Roper and Lucy?"

"From now on," I said, "I have to think about Roper with his head between Lucy's legs, trying to get away from her kooch. And every time I want some jelly on my toast, I'm going to hear Lucy's voice saying, *Lick my jam jar, Daddy, lick my jam jar.* Now if you think that's sick, so be it. All I know is I wish I hadn't been there to hear it."

"I would've kicked his faggot ass so, so bad," Basil said.

"The masturbation thing I get," said Jimmy Sue. "That you couldn't help. But this other thing, it's your own fault."

"What's a lad to do," Dinky said, "when he's living with such a rowdy minx?"

"Keep away from her door when he hears noise behind it," Tina said.

"Like you wouldn't've done the same," Basil said.

"Bellissima!" Jimmy Sue said, and kissed her fingers. Lucille had returned with our tray of margaritas.

"You," I said to Lucille, "are a doll."

"Wait a minute," Basil said, and paused very dramatically, a strained pinch to his face, studying Lucille's wares. "Where is it?"

"Where's what?" she said.

"*You* know."

"No," she said, "I don't."

"The jam jar," said my friend The Prick, taking us into uncharted lands. "You forgot the jam jar!"

Lucille would've dropped the tray had she not already placed it—her eyes had expanded like yawning mouths.

"Pardon me?" she said, Hatchet Lady on her way.

"He's asking," Dinky interrupted, "why you didn't bring the *jam jar*."

"You guys," Tina said. "Don't."

"Yeah," Basil said. "Cause Daddy wants to lick it."

A Rocky-Horror-Picture-Show-Type goobus at the next table over was busy doing magic tricks for his Rocky-Horror-Picture-Show-Type goobus friends, the three of them slouched in their booth with their dyed black hair and big black coats and tight black pants tucked into black Doc Martins and patent leather Beatle boots. They were all glopped up with lipstick and mascara, and Goobus #1, Lord Fascination, had a pink toy dinosaur, Barney, from what I could tell.

"How much do we owe you for the drinks?" I said.

Lucille's eyes were burning. "I thought they were on you," she hissed.

"Did I say that?"

"That must mean you get to lick the jam jar!" Good old Basil. He'd seen my ploy to change the tune and was having not a jot.

"What is this crap, anyway?" Lucille said, playing dumb to the end.

"Come, come, Lucille," Dinky said. "The time for charades has long passed. Andrew Jackson, your roommate, we might remind you, heard the goings-on between you and blubber boy last night."

"Pardon?"

"When was it you forgot how to speak English?" Basil said.

"I heard him, all right. I don't think I understood him."

"Don't even worry about it, Lucy," Tina said. She held up a glass. "Who had salt?"

"Right here," Jimmy Sue said.

"Me, too," I said.

"All right, you bastards. Out with it."

Jimmy Sue stirred her drink and licked a blob of salt from the rim. She wasn't looking at Lucille. "AJ said he heard you with Roper last night."

"But we didn't believe him," Tina said.

"You've got to be kidding. You're kidding, right?"

"Only a miserable twerp like AJ would make up a story like that," said Jimmy Sue.

"It's no big deal really," I said. "Just surprised me is all."

Lucille stood back, her eyes hopelessly, frantically shifting. "You little runt," she said. "You puny little runt."

"Look at him," Jimmy Sue said, pointing my way. "He's shit faced."

"Take it back. Tell them it's a lie."

Tina glared at me. "He's so full of shit." She held up her glass. "Forget about it, Lucy."

"I won't forget about it. What exactly did you tell them?"

"Mommy," Dinky said in his best hot-to-trot vixen's voice, "wants Daddy to lick her jam jar. Please, Daddy, lick it."

"*Maaaaa-mmmyyyy!*" said Basil with his hands out before him like a baby at the breast.

Lucille flicked her smoke into my eye, and then, to The Clash's "Stand By Me," dove across the table screaming, "Liar! liar! liar!"

We fell into a wall hung with ribbons and trophies and pictures of athletes retired. The drinks went flying, in my hair and down my pants—Lucille even took a chunk from my face with her nails. I could see The Rocky-Horror-Picture-Show-Type goobs blurry behind the rest, with their capes and sneers, mumbling stuff like, "She's nothing at all like Pam Grier," and "Violence is so mundane." But Jimmy Sue and Tina got the biggest kick of all. Jimmy Sue's distaste for me I could understand. On a date a few months back, we'd quibbled over sushi at Ibisu, bickered to death the secret of great art, and snarled through choosing the show we'd hit, my pick Monkey Rhythm and The Plimsouls, hers The Misfits and a Sex Pistols wannabe act. When later she announced with a toss of her bob that *Even Cowgirls Get the Blues* was the twentieth century's greatest book, I had to take her home. Tina, on the other hand, unless I could be blamed for having brought her into the Buddy mix way back when, six or seven months before the night in question, and whom I'd recently given a book of Diane Arbus photos for her b-day, hadn't so much as dandruff to put me down. I could hear the two of them cheering Lucille on as she pummeled away. "Fuck him up!" Jimmy Sue cried. "Yeah, Lucy," Tina shouted, "get him!"

In the end some mondo bastard with a vest full of patches dragged us to the street. Next to the Kodak booth on the corner, an ancient bum was hollering at passersby. His old Schwinn bike, a masterpiece, really, had a banana seat and two-foot sissy bar, and ape hangers, too, with long-tasseled grips. The guy was bedecked in leather, head to foot, and sported a helmet from Germany strapped with vintage goggles.

"Now don't spaz out over there," he shouted when he saw us. "If you can't dance, don't start off with the funky chicken!"

The night may have gone sour, but that hadn't kept the gang from stepping out to the tune of *Hatchet Lady!* and *Oh Mommy, Mommy!* and *Daddy still wants to lick the jam jar!* The Trophy Room's neon bathed the street in sad pink light. I thought of Lucille's painting, the woman collapsed in her fruitless world. Her head hung low, Lucille was a spooky premonition.

"For whatever it's worth," I said, "I'm sorry."

Her eyes were mascara ruined by tears. "You didn't have to tell them that."

"I'm really sorry." I tried to put my arm around her, but she shrugged me off and turned away. "Look," I said. "I'll tell them I was lying."

"All you know is little and mean."

"I'll make it up," I said. "Just tell me what to do, and I will."

"Go to hell."

And with that she ran up the Haight, past the bowling alley, past the Mickey D's, and melted into shadows in the park.

"You may think you got over good," Tina said, up in my face for added effect, "but Karma's going to get you."

"You know what you guys are?" Basil said to the girls. "A couple a type-1 morons. Now that," he said with a slap to my back, "was some kind of joke."

"I told you not to tell her."

"It was a joke," Basil said, and slipped a lemon-drop in his mouth. "Forget about it."

The old leather dude was still yammering at the passersby. "I ask you," he shouted at one woman, "if Death Valley is below

LA or to the west of LA, and you don't know. You don't know anything. You're just Mrs Motor Mouth. And you're a messy housekeeper, too!" Then he saw me gaping and said, "You want to know a secret, pal?"

"What's that?"

"Dead men are heavier than Sunday afternoons."

"Yeah?"

"Them and wedding vows."

Dinky, gazing up through the gridlock of muni-wires, still hadn't said a word.

"Tell him, Dink," Basil said.

"Tell him what?"

"That she'll get over it."

"We must always remember old Tom's wondrous words of wisdom," Dinky said, smiling. "*There's nothing wrong with her a hundred dollars won't fix.*"

AUGUST IN THE CAPAY VALLEY IS STRAIGHT-UP death. What water doesn't touch, the sun destroys, the nut trees droop under coats of dust, and the hillsides big with jim brush and sage fret with the shadows of buzzards, and hiding sparrows, and mice. And yet, even so, from a ruin of drought you can walk into corn so dense it might be a wall of scrumptious hair. With dusk the heat resolves—if only faintly, the sky's on you still—until at last night emerges and sleep becomes something you think could be real. That's the rattler's hour, then, time of the skunk, time of the owl, some Achemon sphinx with wings of blood-stained eyes.

For the month since I returned from Portland I've been trucking crops most days and nights to outfits down in Sacto and the Bay, Oaktown mostly, and the veggie quarter south of Frisco. I live in a trailer on cinderblocks, now, with one pair of boots, a pair of cutoffs and two of socks, and an old wool sweater nabbed from Sally-Alley. And save the nip here and there I take with Thomas the Tattooed Whiskey Man, I've quit with the drinking and smoking both. As for the folks who roust me some nights, when the bongos beat and the jug goes round the flames, well, they say I talk in my sleep about a girl by the name of Avey.

It's hard to believe I lived that other life. Not that this one's all that different. I've got nothing to my name but the letters it's made of, them and my rags and the copy of *Fear and Loathing* I stashed in my ruck the day Super got us to the lake. A host of black birds ten thousand strong will rise from a field like a cloud from myth, and it's no more to me than dishes in my sink. I hit the peak of a rise on the road to look down windrows gold as my mother's gold ring, wider and farther than I can tell, and if I don't feel bewildered, it's because I'm numb.

Any boob with sense can see me for what I am. I could care less. Yet when I think on that night, up at Dinky's cabin, waiting for Super to return while Lucille told Hickory I was Satan in the guise of a drunk, how I'd always wanted Lucille for myself but couldn't, not, she said, because I never tried but because she wouldn't have me, how her scorn made me do things no human should have done to a person they called friend, how if Hickory knew what was good she'd get as far from me as her legs could go—when I think of that night from here in the endless quiet heat, I feel I've drunk a bucket of blood. Where Lucille got that stuff, I will never know. Not a snatch of it was true, not the parts that mattered. And besides, what difference did it make, so long as she never tried to load Hickory up with poison? That's how it went: I woke from a nap with a tampon in my tea and her saying she'd found it in some jam.

"It sure does look like one to me," I said. Dinky had sunk back into his pillow. Hickory was glaring. "What exactly did Lucy say?"

She dipped her rag in the basin and sponged Dinky's brow. "You could've told me you were just about anything," she said, "and I'd have believed you."

I'd hoped she'd ask me to explain, or even not to explain, that whatever had happened happened and nothing she or I could do would change it, that even if we could it wouldn't matter, because none of it had happened between us. I wanted her to trust in the promise of the man I was trying to give her. But she dropped her rag and left.

Dinky was snoring. A faint glow had crept into the room. Through the window I watched the swaying trees…

One of the girls had slapped in another disc, I couldn't quite make it out, a wheezing melody, country-like, the lyrics scarcely patchy… *learn how to steer… spill my beer…* Hickory and Lucille were talking—"come back"—"fucking nightmare"—"just those Doritos"… I slipped toward the landing and cocked my head.

"What if they can't get the truck?" Lucille said.

"They'll get it."

"That old man scares me." One glass clinked on another. Something plastic bounced on the table, a lighter or a cup. The couch springs creaked, then the wooden rocker.

"Dinky," Hickory said, "told me you two used to have a thing."

"You think we should be worried about him?"

The music played on… *I don't like riding on the passenger side…*

"I am a little curious, though," Hickory said. "Why'd you leave him?"

"You ever meet someone who'll never say what it is they want? I mean, even when they know it?"

"He says you left him drunk in a fireworks shop. Down in some dirty town in Baja."

"He says that about every woman he's ever had. But really Dinky left himself."

"You and Basil are… Well. You guys can be pretty harsh."

"Buddy Time," Lucille said. "I know, I know. It's hard to understand, especially if you haven't been in it long."

The gnome at my feet was irking me to hell. Everywhere I turned found me challenged by some scrap of carnival, mannequins and clowns and gnomes. You had to wonder what the Wainwrights were about, this family full of tightlipped babbitts who thought they were cool every time they stuck some doll with a boner on their mantle.

"It's funny, you know," Lucille said, "how sometimes things just happen."

"I'm tired of things just happening," Hickory said.

"How things can happen and you don't understand them till after it's too late?"

"And that's if you're lucky."

"It's like when I had that shitty temp job out in Walnut Creek that time," Lucille said. "Ten or so years back, I guess, the summer before I got out of State. I'd taken on this temp job down at Blue Boss Insurance, to make up for what my parents wouldn't cover. Opening mail and photocopying and stuff. There were four of us there, me and this girl named Chiffon-Latrese, and two other bimbos from Antioch. About every three or four days, this guy'd call on the phone. He was a quiet kind of guy. He didn't have any business with the company, that's not why he was calling. He just wanted to hear a woman's voice, he said. It didn't take long to figure out he wanted more than that. Really he was calling to hear our voices while he beat off. He never said that's what he was doing. I just knew it. You could hear him over the line doing his thing, it was kind of loud, and he'd breathe real hard, you know. The thing is, he never said anything nasty to me or anyone else. Two of the girls, the bimbos, they wouldn't talk to him. He'd call and they'd hang up. Only Chiffon-Latrese would talk to him. And me. We felt sorry for him, I guess. Every time I answered it seems like I'd end up talking to him until he was through. You get tired of reading magazines, you know? Chiffon-Latrese, though, she was like me. A temp. Which means after about a month or so she got shipped off to some other shitty hole. Some days the guy would call up and ask me to tell him about my sisters. Some days it was the other women in the office he wanted to know about, what they were doing, that sort of thing. I could always hear him, too, going at it, I mean. But after a couple of weeks he started getting weirder. He asked me to call him names. 'What kind of names,' I said. 'Dirty names,' he said. 'Insult me.' So first I told him he's a good-for-nothing jerk and an asswipe besides, and what did he do but groan and ask for more. I called him a dirty bastard prick and he groans again and starts in with the heavy breathing. I called him a fucking douchebag fuck. I called him a cocksucking piece of dickweed. I called him everything he'd ever read in the *Penthouse* forum, and then some. I was probably getting off on it all more than he was. It was sort of out of hand, I guess, when I really think about it. It had got to the point where I was practically screaming at the top of my lungs when his voice kind of shuddered, and he hung up. The two bimbos were staring at me. It made me think how creepy I must've been. I mean, I was enjoying all of that, you know? It wasn't for about a week or so that the guy called me back. But you know what he does? The first thing he does is ask how big my feet are. I told him I was a tall girl. My feet are bigger than most girls' feet, I said, but they fit my body. He said what size. Ten, I told him, they're size ten. But they fit my body. And then he hung up. Three days later he calls again to say he's been dreaming about me every night, says he's dreaming about my feet. He's been having sex with my feet, he says. I ask what he means by with my feet and he says he's been sticking his dick between my toes after I go to sleep, but that's okay, because that was how we'd planned it. Meaning, in his dream I'd told him the whole thing was cool with me but just to wait till I'd passed out. He asked me if that's okay, that he's been dreaming about me, and I tell him sure, that's okay, why should I care what you do at night. The next time he called, another two or three days'd gone by. He asks if I think he's a pervert. Well look what you've been doing, I say. So I am a pervert, he says. Sure, I say, yeah. But that's okay. It's not like you're stalking me or anything. But I'm a pervert, he says. Everybody's got their thing, I say. And he says, Yes, but I'm a pervert. Then he hung up, and I never heard from him again."

"People do things," Hickory said.

"But you know what?" Lucille said. "I didn't think there was anything wrong with it. I mean, if you really want to know, I thought there was something wrong with *me*. I kept taking his calls. It's like I actually enjoyed talking to him. And when he stopped calling, I missed him. I even got depressed, you know? Every day I'm answering the phone hoping it's my quiet little pervert. One day, after a couple of weeks, I pick up and there's a guy on the end who sounds exactly like my man. I was so obsessed with the whole thing, I'd brainwashed myself into thinking it had to be him. And so in this disgustingly breathy voice I said, *I've missed you, baby*, and the guy says, *Who is this?* Turns out it was just some schmuck calling about his reimbursement. That's when it hit me. *You're* the one who's pathetic, Lucille. You. Fucking pathetic."

The girls were quiet then. I went back to Dinky. His breathing was still bad, and he was sweating and gibbering again, this freaky thing after that. The wreck must've busted him up inside, the way he carried on. Sure, he was sick before we'd got here, but not like that. Or maybe he'd always been sick but just never said. Or maybe he'd never said because he wanted us to see for ourselves, to say something, maybe, as if we cared, to console or advise him—it was there before our eyes, wasn't it, plain as a bomb going off?—or maybe just to ignore it altogether, anything so long as it wasn't this elephant-in-the-living-room type scene we all made light of in that lily-livered way of ours, when things got too heavy for anything else. He wanted something pure, I imagine, something he could count on.

I sat down beside him, wondering what I could do to make it go away. Spittle had pooled at the corners of his mouth. I wrung out the cloth from the basin and placed it on his brow. Once again he began to weep. I looked away, out toward the advancing dawn, and watched a list of stillicides trickle from the eaves…

*A sphere of glass filled with plastic snow. A withered hand clutching the sphere until it slipped and shattered on the marble floor. Rosebuds across a carpet, yellow, white, and red…*

Downstairs I paused in the landing this side of the door, and peered around the corner. Hickory lay on the couch, fooling with a Rubik's Cube. Lucille had propped herself up by a bourbon at the table to doodle on a napkin.

"It's pretty bad, huh?" Lucille said.

"You saw him yourself," Hickory said.

"But you don't know him like I do. I've seen him this way a hundred times."

"Still."

Lucille slapped the pen down and gulped at her drink. "Maybe the phone'll start working."

"Maybe," Hickory said.

"He shouldn't have let himself get that way."

"Maybe we should try and grab some sleep."

"He'll be fine."

"I could use some of that." I went to the table and poured myself a shot. The girls wore faces so thick they could've been spirits from an ancient play. At a low, nearly subliminal volume, Black Francis with his half-scream/half-croon kept repeating his line. *It is time, it is time, it is time for stormy weather.* "Is that some kind of joke?" I said, and killed the sound.

"Ode," Lucille said.

"What?"

"It's supposed to be ironic," Hickory said.

"You're just pissed," Lucille said, "because of that time Black Francis said he wanted to cut your ponytail off."

This was true. We'd gone to Smarts, this trendy LA hole you could spot a handful of stars in any given day. One night we found Uma Thurman, Johnny Depp, and Ethan Hawke playing pool together, drunk as goons in a depot. The night in question we'd run across Black Francis—AKA Frank Black, AKA Charlie Thompson—hiding in a corner, scowling with his porcine eyes. I had a ponytail then, like Lucille said. What Lucille did not say was how I'd whipped it into Charlie's face and told him I had to take a shit.

"Black Francis," I said, "is a pudgy glob of snot with a tude."

"You," Lucille said, "were just too much of a puss to say anything to him. Basil would've kicked his ass."

"Basil would've eaten his ass clean out if he'd thought it would get him somewhere."

"He'll kick *your* ass the second he gets back and I tell him about all the smack you're talking."

"He can eat my ass, too. Just like you. Eat my ass."

"Maybe you children could save it?" Hickory said.

"Don't look at me," Lucille said.

"She sure as hell isn't going to look at me," I said.

Hickory started toward the stairs. "I'm going to lie down."

Lucille and I sat there twiddling, furious in our ineptitude.

"We're pretty sorry, all right," I said.

"All I want is to get the hell out of this dump."

"Whatever I've done to get on your bad side, I'm sorry."

"Payback's a bitch, ain't it?"

"Have it your way. But remember. You've got to deal with it till we're gone."

"You've got nothing, AJ. No life, nothing. If I thought otherwise, I'd say you make me sick."

I shuffled across the room like a freshly spanked child and stopped before a penny on the carpet. Old Abe's face in copper profile must've done something to me, because from out of nowhere, like some cat in a game show from Mars, I was swirling in a vortex of happenstance and quirk: Lincoln was elected president in 1860, Kennedy in 1960. Both were slain on Fridays, in the presence of their wives, both were shot in their imperial skulls. John Wilkes Booth was hatched in 1839, Lee Harvey Oswald in 1939. Lincoln had a gofer named Kennedy, Kennedy one named Lincoln… Yes, yes—and the hip bone's connected to the leg bone. One bygone Christmas, before the looney tunes had stepped up to conk her, my grandmother gave me a two dollar bill, a Pet Rock, and a book of disco dance steps, including the Bionic Boogie, the Weekend Two-Step, and Le Freak. Last year, on Christmas Day, in a drunken tango down Waller Street with a girl named Date, I fell to the walk before a makeshift sign of bamboo and cardboard, its words scrawled with a paintbrush in the hand of a child: On December 24th THIS DATE PALM WAS STOLEN BY A SHORT WHITE MALE WITH SHOULDER LENGTH BROWN HAIR MERRY X-MAS DIRT BALL! And Lucille Ball's all-time favorite show was M*A*S*H, and Amos Alonzo Stagg, AKA The Masher, invented the football dummy in 1889. Scat of the opossum, a beast that plays dumb when scared, is called werderobe, scat of the otter, spraints. The Yokut Indians used dust of spraints mixed with a liquor derived from the coffee bush to rid minds possessed by an odious spirit from the lands of thunder song and rattles. And while Jelly Roll Morton died believing he'd been cursed by a voodoo witch, Hippocrates ushered medicine from the realm of muddled superstition. Love is superstition, superstition, danger. Danger is an owl in the night.

SPC Stuyvesant Wainwright, IV
B Co 16th En Br
Operation Joint Endeavor
APO AE 09789
5 Feb 96

Dear Andrew Jackson Harerama vanden Heuvel

How are you my night-owlish friend? I've not heard any news from you since before you took on that job at State. Write to me and tell me what your plans are for the future.

I got a Christmas card from Jacquelyn and she said you weren't seeing each other anymore. But that was two months ago. I'm sure things may have changed by now. I wrote Basil about him breaking up too and said we could be 3 bachelor amigos when we get back. But I'm sure your situations will have changed by then.

Life here in Bosnia is usually boring but occasionally dangerous. The first American just died yesterday—the papers/news media are filled with speculation as to how. Military intelligence has informed us that he went out to take a shit (right off the road). He was squatting down and saw something in the ground. He took his Leatherman pocket pliers and poked at it. The medics found half his leatherman embedded in his brain! Lovely, huh?

Yesterday I spent all ~~night~~ day burning shit. 9-1/2

hours to burn 1/2 barrel of shit and piss. It is a smelly, shitty detail but somebody has to do it. Ha ha. We pour diesel into the 1/2 barrel (which sits below the bench in the 3-seater latrine) and stir it up. Then we light it and stir it constantly. Sounds like fun, huh? I can't wait for a job with a desk, buddy!

Buddies forever,

Stuyvesant

It was all too horribly true…

I had no money, I had no power, Lord of the Latrines I was, Prince of the Pubes, credentials alone to have got me elected President of the Cult of the Fool. How does such a man break out like wild dogs, much less like a parakeet? How does such a man give his ghosts the bodies they've lost, much less make them bleed?

Next to the bath, the cabin had two upper rooms. Dinky was unchanged, mumbling his flow of applesauce and bile. I groped my way into the second room, fixed on purging myself and the girl in it of the germs that kept us low.

*Tweet, tweet, tweet, my darling, tweet, tweet, tweet!*

*And the moments, dear, look how fast, look how lithe and fleet!*

MOST NIGHTS I LAY ON MY COT PICKING PETALS off imaginary daisies and conjure visions of those hours with Avey May Jones, of how as she melted to my words it struck me she'd grant my wish at last and give both body and words to me in return, if not forever then for what was left of that one sad night. All my life I'd dreamed of finding her. For all those days and all those years she'd been the knot of my dreams, my honeyed lump of winter mud, my mud song, simple, warm. I wanted to get stuck in her, all right. I wanted to stay that way forever…

I told her what had happened the time I came home to find Roper and Lucille. I told her what had happened at the Trophy Room, too, when Dinky and Basil had opened their can of fucked-up worms and set high the bar of mutilation. Then I told her the story of my wicked worthless life, of everything I'd thought I knew myself to be, who I was and where I'd been, and where I'd wanted to go and be. Had I tried to present myself as anything more than pitifully pitiful, she'd probably have abandoned me on the spot. However foolish I'd been till then, I was smart enough in those few moments to know my limits. The only thing worse than denying you're pitiful is to act it while you are.

"Nothing I told you tonight was the truth," she said. I'd just finished up my tale of squalor and abuse. "About myself, I mean. When we were playing Truth or Dare."

"Not even your name?"

"Naming something is the fastest way I know to screw it up."

"I don't think I believe that."

"Name a thing, you strangle it."

"You must've had a reason."

"I grew up in a dusty little town with a state mental hospital and a Boss Hogg-type cattle baron. My dad worked for the county fixing potholes and signs."

"Bet your mom dug that."

"Dead people don't dig anything I'm aware of."

"Before that, I mean, if there was a before."

"I never knew one way or another how she felt about anything. And what I do remember isn't much fun."

"I guess that's the problem, huh? How much we need our memories, but hate ourselves for the needing and having both?"

Hickory went to the bureau with Dinky's family photos. When she turned back, I knew she was going to spin a yarn.

"We lived at the outskirts of town. Out by the hills. There weren't many houses there. Just a couple of adobe bungalows and a big metal barn they used for storing hay. Daddy did side work for the guy who owned it. He was an old guy with a bunch of cars Daddy fixed on weekends. Anyhow, one day when I was six or seven the school had a bomb threat. Somebody called up and said they were going to kill every kid in town, and they sent us home. I'd gone in through the back, by the garage, to scrounge around the kitchen for something to eat. But just as I was turning on the TV I heard voices from the back of the house. Most days Mom was never home, she had a part-time job some place, I don't know what or where, so at first the voices scared me.

"I snuck around the corner. You know how you get when you're a kid and something breaks down your notions of the way things are? No one had ever been in the house during the day except for my mom. But this was a man's voice. I didn't know whose it was. I just knew it wasn't Daddy's. The man was laughing. Not loud. Soft, but different than Daddy's kind of soft. The hallway was dark. Up and down the walls we had these family photos, all the usual thieves. Most were people I'd never met, old men and women with eyes like eyes in daguerreotypes. I'd seen them all so many times it'd got to where I didn't notice them any more. But that day all I could do was stand beneath them, watching them watch me with those eyes.

"I can't remember how long I stood there while the man kept laughing. It never got louder or softer. Every once in a while the woman said something I couldn't understand. It didn't sound like my mom, though, though I knew it was her. I must've done something, maybe scraped the wall, because my dog Blinky-Doo started barking, and then he came trotting round the corner. That's when the man stopped laughing. 'Is someone here?' he said, and my mom said, 'Hello?' but I didn't answer.

"Next thing I heard was a mumble of whispers and scratchy sounds. Blinky-Doo was licking my face. Then I looked up, and my mom was there with messy hair and her face all smeared, wearing an open robe. The man I'd remembered seeing before, at some store in town or just on the street. He had hair all over his belly and chest. His shirt was unbuttoned, and he had a mustache, that much I remember, too. I thought he was going to say something, but he just looked at me till after a while he left.

"'They made me come home early,' I told my mom. 'You little sneak,' she said. 'I wasn't,' I said. My mom's eyes, I realized, were glued to my dress. It was hot and wet, and so was the carpet. 'If you don't tell your daddy what you saw today,' she said, 'I won't tell him what you just did.'"

"I hate people," I said. "Sometimes I do."

"I never did tell him."

"If I ask you something," I said, "will you tell me?"

"Depends."

"What did they call you, your mom and dad?"

"The name on my birth certificate says Avey May Jones. But the day I was born, when I was still in the hospital, the nurse who brought me out to Daddy said, *She's the sweetest little mud patty I've ever seen*, and Daddy said, *Hello, Mud. I'm your daddy*. From then on out it's been Mud."

"She said that? That's like, I don't know, like stuff from fairytales and film."

"Like stuff that happens in little towns with insane asylums and slaughterhouses."

"She really said that?"

"I can only guess it's because Daddy's half-black. His mother was the only black woman in Ft Smith married to a white man. That's how they came out here. Nobody could stand it, her practically being made into a whitey."

"My name is Mud," I said. "I like that."

"You like it?"

"Like is not the word."

We were on the bed. She was holding my hand, without fear or pretense, as if really and truly it was something she'd wanted as much as I. Her breath smelled like bourbon and ginger and peach and smoke, the soul of an antique dream. I could see the smallest hairs above her lip. A vein ran along her jaw, just below her ear, in her evening-colored skin, the faintest pulsing blue.

"What?" I said.

I know it couldn't have really been that way, but that's the way

I imagined it, or thought I'd imagined it, because I thought I imagined she kissed me. Her breath smelled of mountains, then, and of butterfly dust, and of the feathers of quiet birds. The sound of her heart came up through her mouth, I could taste it, too, the sound of her heart, a morsel of chocolate, laughing. She took my face in her hands, she held my face as though at any moment it might explode. Her hair fell across my face, and she closed her eyes, and I felt it again, the first time since forever, brand-spanking-new. That goddamned girl—that's what she did—she made it all feel so shiny and new.

We didn't know it then, or maybe we did, fuck it, but we were only using each other, hiding in each other the fates of our broken selves, all those years of hope and dread. *Call-notes of dark sobbing*, sang Rilke. And that's what it was, that love, impossible to swallow…

I ran my hands along her neck, her shoulders and smallish breasts. A tattoo circled her navel, a sun with rays of purple and black, and I made a circle over that. There was only the wind and rain…

The clock on the stand said 4:32, Wednesday, December 31st, New Year's Eve: the beginning of an end, the end of a beginning, more than ninety hours since any of us had known a wink of sleep.

Avey and I were silent with our new misunderstanding, which was all we could ever have been…

The smell of us was strong in that mountain air, my breath on her neck, dying…

My having made this girl had only put us further apart. A pinhead of black had crept into my bowels, but then the sandman came, and I was taken with a sigh…

THE SUN HAD RISEN BY THE TIME THAT TREE slammed through the cabin, but neither Avey nor I had heard it. I thought of disbelieving Basil's claim to've slept through those tornadoes in Kansas, after the funeral of a chain-smoking cousin.

"Everybody was in the same room," he said. "Six or seven of my great uncles and aunts and fifty thousand cousins."

"Baloney," I said.

"Try staying up for five days of drinking and snorting," he said, "before topping it off with a funeral. See how fast you come to."

We were hanging at the Mallard, waiting to play pool. Down the bar Dinky and some other boobs were deep in a game of liar's dice. Basil took an ice cube and bopped it off our friend's titanic head.

"Hey, O'Connor," Dinky shouted to the bartender.

"Now what?" O'Connor said, cramming his brush into a glass.

"We thought we'd agreed to 86 that blowhard next time he started up with his shenanigans."

Basil leaned over the bar to better yell at Dinky. "Just making sure that sack of concrete you call a head was still hard enough for me to knock around at pool, Dink. Serious," he said, back at me. "I was eight sheets to the wind."

"But that didn't keep you from making a good show for the familia, I'll bet."

"Three tornadoes in a row—blam, blam, blam—one right after the next."

"So how is it then you're still around to tell the tale?"

"Hit every house but ours, cross my heart. Motherfucking Godzilla could've smashed through the walls, having it out with Mothra, and I wouldn't've heard dick."

It wasn't until an incoherent rant had broken through my dreams, like a siren in the distance, that I suspected something wrong. Avey nuzzled into me, the smell of her restful, kind, and mumbled that Lucille ought to shut it. The world was suspended in haze—the rose-patterned linen, the vase on the floor, the print of a goat on a craggy spire, gazing toward a stretch of valleys and arêtes. I wanted to stay in that haze, for a while at least, and in the shelter of Avey's hair, but the storm raged about us, and the voice went on.

"Get down here, you guys," Lucille was shouting. "Hurry!"

Avey shuffled along beside me, drowsy at the rail. Then we saw the carnage, and snapped sober in a beat. Half the front of the cabin had collapsed into the living room, crushed by a giant pine.

Lucille looked as we'd left her, a drink in this hand, a smoke in that.

"Murphy's Law," Avey said.

"What?" Lucille said.

"Whatever can go wrong," I said, "will."

The tree hadn't crushed the living room alone, but most of the deck, besides. Good thing for us old Granddad Wainwright had had the wits to hire craftsmen, not the jerks you see today, wobbling round some rafter fifty-feet up, guzzling a frosty as they slice off their ruined hands. None of that, though, meant we could stay.

"I guess they haven't made it back," I said.

"I only wanted to have a good time before my life was over," Lucille said, crying. "Nothing big or fancy, you know?"

"Put on your jacket."

"What?" she said.

Avey made her way to a pile of clothes near the hearth and picked out Lucille's jacket.

"Come here," I said.

"What?" Lucille said, rooted to the spot with her washed-out face. I stepped through the wreckage and hugged her as she cried like you do when you don't know who you are.

"I'm sorry," she said. "I'm sorry. Can't we just, I don't know… *go?*"

"Let's get your jacket on," I said. "We'll get your jacket on and fix a little something up for your belly."

"Promise me you'll get us out of here."

"Put your jacket on."

"Promise me, AJ."

"If Basil and Super get here soon," Avey said, "we stand a chance of hitting Berkeley in time to sing 'Auld Lang Syne.'"

"Did either of you happen to bring an umbrella?" I said.

"By the door," Lucille said.

"I'm going out."

"Maybe we should check on Dink," Lucille said.

"Let him sleep," I said. "You two head upstairs and kick it till I'm back."

North and south the road lay slick with mud, worse in the light of day than I'd imagined it last night. With Lucille's absurd umbrella, semé with smiley faces—yellow, naturally—I went the way of Basil and that freak of a man, hoping round the bend to meet some crew, but found just more desolation. Long minutes passed before a figure appeared at the end of the road, who, it didn't matter: I wanted news from the world, that was all. But the harder I looked, the greater it seemed the figure to be more beast than man, Sasquatch meets the Scarecrow. It was only after I'd decided to take cover that a man called out, and I knew that it was Basil.

"Where's Super?" I said.

My pal sat down with dangling arms, his feet, both bare, a mass of sores. "That old fucking fuck," he said. "He tried to take a razor to my ass."

Basil unhurt that I could see left me unsure what to say. "So then you never made it to his wheels."

"I said I needed to rest. But you know what he does? He starts in with one of those psycho rants. When I told him to cut the crap, dude came up with a razor. And that dog of his. Turned into frigging Cujo."

"He was helping us. He needed your help with the truck."

Basil picked a twig from his foot. He was virtually in tears. "A hundred times I tried to tell you."

"Are you all right?"

"Sure, AJ," he said, "I'm fine. In just a second here I'm going to jump up and sing in all this rain."

"You must've really pissed him off."

"Attacked him with a hatchet's all."

"Dude, he took you down and laughed. The man's a vet for Christ sake."

"He's a psychopath is what he is, AJ."

"I don't know."

"Go ahead then, tit. Believe what you want. All I know is he and his beast came at me like gangbusters."

"And then he let you skate."

"The old caveman combo."

"Let's just hope he comes back."

"He does, it won't be to bring us flowers."

"He liked us, Baze. He did me and Dinky, at least."

"Goddamn it. Goddamn it, goddamn it, goddamn it."

"Think you can make it to the cabin?"

"I am so very fucking done, AJ, you don't even know."

I got Basil to his feet and his arm round my neck. "I forgot to tell you."

"Don't even mess with me, okay?"

"A tree kind of smashed up the cabin."

"Goddamn it. Godfuckingdamn it."

We limped up the road. Minutes passed before we spoke.

"You're a good guy," Basil said.

"I try."

Before the spectacle of the cabin, Basil's face went rubbery and helpless and gleeful and sour, none of it for long. A face of horror took him, then, and then again he began to weep.

"You guys polish off the hooch?" he managed to say.

"We got some hooch, I think."

"Because I want them to find us like a jar full of top drawer fucking pickles."

"The old man's coming back, you know. He said he was coming back."

My friend was shaking now, too, nearly uncontrollably, his feet might've been stuffed through an old-school grinder. He gazed up at the cabin and shook his head.

"Looks like Godzilla came through here," he said.

"It's true," I said. "Him and Mothra both."

IT OCCURRED TO ME AS WE MOUNTED THE STAIRS that Dinky wouldn't have to engineer a story for his grandfather about the window Basil smashed. The birdcage was there, caging a bird that was dead. I scooped the cage up with Lucille's umbrella and tossed them in the mud.

Inside, with no lights or music to make a cheery fiction, everything was cloaked in grey—dripping water, trembling prints, shadows and slime and shit.

"So now the power's cut, too, I take it," Basil said.

"Yup."

"Where is everybody?"

"Last I checked the girls were upstairs in bed."

"I just want to go home."

"We need a plan."

"But we can't go home. Because we are fucking stuck."

"I say we take what we can carry and go."

"Like a pack of tittysucking rats."

"I'm serious, dude."

"Denial ain't a river in Egypt, Jackson." He looked at me now with gravity I'd never seen. For the first time in his life he was trying to be real. "You smell me, or what?"

I sat on the bench and lit a smoke and handed it to Basil, then lit one for myself.

"I wish to God I couldn't," I said.

"And I wish to God you could understand me for once. You know that?"

"No, I don't. I've got no idea what you mean."

"Of course you don't. You never do, and never have. You've never understood a thing about me."

"We get ourselves out of here in one piece," I said, and grinned, "I promise we can go to counseling. How's that sound?"

"I love you, too," Basil said. "So, *so* much."

Lucky for us he'd remembered to bring his suitcase in before Dinky and I wrecked his Cruiser. We stripped our clothes and argued over who'd wear what. Basil pointed at my shriveled up dong and asked how I'd gotten a shroom to grow in my crotch. I called him a rich boy. I called him a monkey-fucking banana dick. Then I put on one of his dress shirts, with the French cuffs and polka dots, and a red velvet vest over that, and lo and behold, I looked like a numbskull in the hand-me-downs of his brother the mime. Basil went to see about the girls.

In its way the earth had gone quiet, the solemn trees, the heaving sky. Veils of rain continued to fall, the lake was hidden, there was only mud, only trees and sky. But soon a woman cried out, and soon another began to scream, Lucille louder than Avey at first, though presently they were wailing as one, cries with pain enough to rend the hardest man, ah, exactly what we needed. Hardly had I thought to investigate than Basil stood beside me again, his face as long and blue as ever a face could be.

He lifted me off the ground and squeezed till I lost my breath. I could feel him shaking, his whole body in tremors, ambushed by a life of hurt. It was only some years later, or so it seemed, that he gave in, his voice a boom in my ear, nothing comprehensible. Shaking and sobbing, he just held me tight.

"He's dead, AJ. I went in to see him… He was just *dead*."

Basil said that, and his face dropped away like a coin off a cliff. I fell dizzy with pictures of catheters and cotton and chromium rails, and screens above flowers and sirens, too, host after host, and widowers and widows, the injustice of their eyes, and needles, and hoses, and smocks, and tubes…

A hand lay on my brow, cool as a spring, I could smell Avey's breath and hair. We lay on the bed we'd slept in, a cheap coverlet scratching at my jaw. An old chiffonier stood across the room with its small brass tub of imitation flowers. Next to it was a smattering of novels from the World's Best Reading and a painting of Jesus in a dime store frame. Lucille was perched on a cedar chest, her arms around her knees. Basil sat beside me, with a smoke.

"Are you okay?" Avey ran her fingers through my hair, they were light and soft.

"Where is he?"

"Sssshhhh."

I looked into her eyes. I nuzzled in her hair. "I'm okay. I'm fine."

Basil went to Lucille, he held Lucille's hand. They were silent.

"Where is he?"

"In there," Lucille said.

For a moment the room seemed crooked, everything floaty with mist. Then it cleared, and I was on my feet, steady as could be by Avey, her hand on my leg.

There was a door.

I went in. By the bed I got down. I got down on my knees. But I did not look. Not at him, his face. I couldn't. For a long time I sat that way…

His face. Not his face…

No can. Maybe never, maybe not never, not knowing when, maybe never…

Laid there, he, it, he, a cold stiff thing, stretched out like a dummy, CPR, a hand, not like his face had been, not jaundiced, not sweaty and pained, hands of a workman never done work, no not. And fingers, thick, blunt at the tips, where thick hard nails were growing still, no, not growing, not life, never again, not, no, no pulseless mush but veins, and blue cording, and thick-ish veins, ah, heavy, ah, like ugly crappy wire. Little blond hairs not vanished, no not, no not, and thousands of hole-dots, and lines connect dots, not color in, no not, no not, no not, design, no design, no not, never, nothing, no, where wrinkles there, and cold, so cold, hand in hand, so cold, so cold, no not, not, not, not think meat, not think friend, not friend, not think, no not, no nothing there, nothing, no, not, no, no, no, no, not, no not, no not not, not, not. And you will look, now, yes, you will look. At him. At not him, at not it but him, but Dinky, look at him, no, look at him, yes, you, now, yes, because, because, because. And there, yes, and there now, and there. And it's okay, you are there, you are fine, it's okay, it is okay, everything's okay, it is…

Peaceful is not the word. Dinky's face was not peaceful. That, I thought, was the big untruth, this business of peace suffusing the dead. But though it looked nothing at all like peace, my friend's lifeless face, neither did it look sad, nor helpless, nor anguished, nor anything of the sort. Content, perhaps. Or perhaps *nothing* is more like it. More like it, yes, Dinky had a face of nothing, a face no longer burdened, with worry, with fear, with anything to speak of, desire, anger, rage—that was all.

I wiped my mouth. I wiped my eyes. My fingers shook, and my hand. But then I made that hand touch him, his face, his mouth, his eyes, everything he'd been, my damp hand on his dead face, which wasn't cold but cool. And that was all. It rested there, I let it, my hand on his brow, and then I began to sob, and everything left me, all my thoughts and all my words swallowed up by that good cry. You son of a bitch, you, you beautiful mother fucker, you, who couldn't stand another day. I pulled the sheet to his chin and made it straight. I shouldn't thank you, I thought, but I can't help it. Thank you, Dinky, thank you, Stuyvesant Wainwright, IV. And then I pulled the sheet over his face and smoothed it again, and then I said, *Thank you, again*, I said, *thank you*... *Yes*, I said, *thanks*, I said, *you old bastard, thanks.*

THE WAY WE LOVE THE DEAD'S GOT NOTHING TO do with how we love the living.

I'd be hauling down some road with a mackerel sky against the dawn, watching crows in the fields or egrets in rice, and like fear it would hit me I couldn't go home expecting his voice on the line whenever I called, rambling about the game he'd just bought or the stripper he'd had that photo-op with, with the massive tits she let him squash his face into while the cameras ticked and flashed. Or before that, before I'd moved to these podunk lands, when I was still a sofa-surfer, tripping place-to-place with my bag of books, I'd be hanging at the Strada or Milano, watching the students and the freaks, the little rich daddy's girls, the hard-nosed punks shouting for coin enough to make them puke, the date-rape jug heads and beret-wearing doofs with their euro smokes and foreign mags, and it would hit me, uncanny as hell, the friend I thought I'd known like the day, different every time, saying or doing what I couldn't recall him saying or doing while he was yet alive.

The only thing sure I could say about Dinky was he'd taken off for that whorehouse in the sky—that and how every time I thought of him, I was loving him. But the Dinky of my eulogies had no part in the Dinky I had known. The Dinky of my eulogies was the Dinky of my grief, the Dinky of my heart gone soft.

He was never the kid I'd witnessed barfing off a terrace, the kid with a bag of speed grumbling about the law, who cringed at the thought of his father, wanting nothing more than to satisfy the man, at whatever cost to his own small needs. The sob stories he used to spew had lapsed into murk the moment he had himself. And even if he did resemble that, it wasn't his fault. Always he floated before me as the angel done wrong. He'd lost his way among the dangers of this shithole world, then found himself in a haunted house. The cards had turned up cold. The cookie had crumbled on another guy's plate, the milk was forever spilling. The only way he could get what mattered most—a simple embrace, just acceptance, just love—was to die. Well, now he'd got his wish. I can't speak for his family, but I can for us buddies: Dinky died, and we were sorry, and we loved the son of a bitch now like we never had while he was here to take it.

From time to time I'd think on this, late at night, in the grip of my insomnia. The cicadas would whir. The great horned owls, six syllables to the hoot, would softly, repeatedly call. In the heat of a furnace-like noon, dreaming at the wheel, I'd think about it then, as well, and I'd hate us all in our cock-eyed ways.

Maybe it's wrong to love the dead. Maybe that kind of love is nothing but the product of our selfish wants, unguent of grief, salve of messy guilt. But what are the options? Should I have committed myself to a life with the monks for not doing right by my friend? Flopped myself down on an old prie-dieu and waited for the Word? It's not as though I'd intended this, this morbid, useless love. It's not as though I'd needed Dinky dead before I could give him his deserts. Now and again, though, when the trick's all said and done, you find yourself left with nothing to say but *That's the way it is.* You can talk a lot of dirt in this world, everyone knows, but you can never say the way we love the dead's got thing one to do with how we love the living.

THE LITTLE GNOME WAS GLEAMING ITS HORRIBLE joy when I stepped into the hall. I kicked its face and watched it blow down the stairs in a dust of plaster and paint…

Some human outside was whistling, "Blue Moon," the reason far beyond. But out on the deck I understood: Super had returned with Fortinbras the dog. And yet something wasn't right. Super, Fortinbras, Fortinbras, Super: nothing but a weird old man like rags on a stick—him and his henchman, and through the trees the mist on the lake.

"You got the truck?" I said.

Super had seen our disaster—he must have—and yet he was smiling. Here was a man who'd part for confusion every time. Here was a man who loved what was toppled, broken, spinning, and cracked, the man with the hands of ink and bone, the man with the monkey, the impervious match. O give me a plain where the wild things grow, give me a spread of broken dolls, O give me a national anthem.

"It's as clear to us as a mountain spring that you smell this business with a dead man's nose."

"You think that's cute?" I said.

"All right, all right, soothe yourself, now. Our wheels we do have."

"That's good, Super, cause Stuyvesant is dead."

For the briefest of instants the old man assumed a pose so brittle it seemed impossible to contain. He might've been seized by some grotesque rash of meaning, a thing with talons and fangs, whose sole purpose was to hurl us through the void. He pulled out a watch and wound it so long I thought surely it would break. But then he stopped and looked into my eyes and let fall the watch to crush with his heel.

"Come on in," I said. "As a favor to Dinky."

The mannequin lay in a twist of stuff and tree. Bits of glass dully spangled, spears of wood harshly jutted, the mobile clinked, the curtains flapped, the cabin creaked and groaned. The rain had ceased for a time. Beads of grey plopped and plopped, from a dangling wire, a frond of fir, that stupid-ass Mexican boner-doll.

The old man's eyes traveled the room with a helplessness he hadn't yet revealed. It wasn't the cabin's state that had got him, I thought, so much as what it stood for. The place could've gone up like Sodom and Gomorrah, as long as Dinky didn't watch. But Dinky had watched, and now, leastwise for Super, he'd become a pillar of salt. The geeze held my shoulder. His face drew near, so close his beard touched my chin, and hovered there infused with the grief in an old seal's eye, perhaps, or the wisdom of a puppy. I began to weep again.

"We know this concern," he said. "We've been where there is to be and seen what there is to see."

The tears were coming so hard it was difficult to stay with Super's words.

"Like we said, the world's gone flat. Days'll come and go and leave you shy of a whit of sun—of that you can be sure. But so long as you're living you ain't broke. No matter what you do, you can only go so low. You bend, you give, you give some more and then you bend again. And just when you think you've got to where you can't go no more, you find yourself giving another pinch of sand, bending another inch. And then you twist back up and start from the get. You might want to, boy, trust him, old Super knows, but you couldn't break if you tried. You're too tiny."

The old man stepped off with a face of good and held me till I laughed.

"What are we going to do?"

"We'll take care of the Wainwright boy."

I'd forgotten about Avey and the others. I thought of what Basil had said, that he'd wanted the old man dead.

"I'd better go let them know you're here."

"You do that. And when you're finished, we'll be waiting."

The crew had by now fully zonked. I shut the door and whispered. No one stirred. I kneeled at Avey's side, I stroked her hair, I gazed into her sleeping face. She murmured. Then I kissed her, and she murmured like before.

"Super's back," I said. "Wake up."

"I don't want to," she said.

I kissed her face. I kissed her eyes, her mouth, her nose. "All we've got to do is make it to the truck." When she stirred again, Basil jerked to with screwy eyes.

"Calm yourself," I said.

"Where you been?"

"Listen. You do something stupid, you could really botch it up."

"He's back?"

"Yes."

Basil tried to stand, but couldn't. "Son of a bitching mother fucking shit!" he said as he collapsed.

I felt for him, a little. The guy couldn't make any more trouble for Super now than he could for the pope. Of course this commotion had pressed our beauties to another go at life.

"What's wrong?" Lucille said.

"His feet are all messed up."

"That's why you woke us?"

"The old man," Basil said. "He's back."

"With the truck I hope."

"Yup," I said.

Lucille jumped. "What are we waiting for?"

"Super's going to help us with Dinky. Okay?"

"You just make sure," Basil said, taking up his bottle, "that that fiend ain't pulling a fast one."

Super appeared at the door. He looked at the girls and said, "Hello, butterflies."

"Don't take this personally," Lucille said, "but I thought you had a truck."

"It's up the road," I said.

"That," Basil said, "is where he and his beast are going to chop us into suey."

"Now, now, Laertes," Super said, and extended a bony hand, "we were hoping there'd be no armored sentiments here."

"My sentiments're armored all right. I don't feel a thing."

"Come on," I said. "Shake his hand."

"I don't want to shake his hand."

I couldn't believe it. The lunk was positively sulking. "Basil. The man is helping us."

"You can stay here if you want to, lover," Lucille said. "You want to stay here?"

"I'm like an elephant. I never forget." Basil sat there blinking. His head was swaying, a balloon on a string. We watched him. "What the hell," he said, and gave his hand. "If it'll make you tits all happy."

"You're a good boy, Laertes. Fortinbras said so on the hump. We're sorry you had to learn that way."

"Was he really that much trouble?" Lucille said.

"We never did know the meaning of that word."

"I only meant," Lucille said, "he didn't mean any harm." In her voice I heard desperation. The time had long passed for rudeness with the geeze who for some crazy reason had kept on coming back. "We just want to go home."

"The sooner we get to the wheels, the sooner you'll not be here."

"*So*," Avey said.

No one had to probe her gist. Her gaze had wandered toward Dinky's room. Basil hit the bottle. Lucille picked her lip.

"We take it that's where you're weeping for the Wainwright boy," Super said.

"How is it you plan to get him out of here?" Basil said.

"We can help," Lucille said. She looked at Avey.

"You two help Basil," I said. "We'll get Dinky."

"What," Basil said, "you think he somehow lost a hundred and fifty pounds?"

"I can carry my half," I said, "if he can carry his."

"We can carry him and his coffin if needs be," Super said.

"AJ," Basil said as he drew near. "You really think the old man's square?"

"He takes us into town, I don't care what the fuck he is."

Basil looked out through the ruins, his features hardening. "Right," he said.

*Pink Champagne Bitch* lay by Dinky, next to some bottles and a tray full of butts. A wad of bubblegum stuck to the nightstand. A pair of socks poked from under the bed. There was a wet and stinking pea coat, two shitty sneakers, a bag stuffed with underwear and shirts and a worthless belt. And shaving cream, and toothpaste, and lotion, and a pack half-empty of Camel Lights, and those stinking awful clowns.

When Super pulled down Dinky's blanket, I expected eyes like pinballs staring through the cold. But someone had come in and put a ski cap over his face, which I removed and placed on my head. And his face *was* cold, and his eyes *were* pinballs, blind as pinball chrome. Maybe that was good. Who could say what Dinky saw on the other side? Maybe little nymphs with paper wings, or hobgoblins and beetles and fire and heath, and the flesh of sinners peeling from bones. And anyway, who the hell really cared? I only knew what he wouldn't be seeing, what he'd never dream again. Not the tsunamis of December or the tippy-tip toes of a gorgeous ballerina. He'd never once, not ever again, see a hatchling from its egg, a leaf on a breeze, chocolate on a shelf in the sun. Women would fight with their men in tenemental gloam, and trout would flop on the fishmonger's board. And masons would trowel, and strippers dance, and bankers bank, but Dinky, he wouldn't know it, because, turning to dirt like a rabbit in the woods, he wasn't any more now than the dream of the dreamer dreaming. If only it were easy as saying, *Arrivederci, pal, and good luck. I'll toss one back when there's land in sight.* Goddamn, but one thing's sure—there's not a stitch of glory in death.

"How far did you say it was to the truck?"

"It ain't. You take his feet and we'll get his head."

I didn't think it right we cart Dinky off like a sack of dirt. We had to wrap him up first, at least. That's what I told Super, and he agreed. I took down the blanket and rolled him. He was heavy as a block of steel. And all along his backside, ankles to groin, his skin had mottled up in a swirl of purples and blues. It looked as if he'd been lying for weeks in a pool of wine.

The flesh beneath the hair on his legs was cool. I could've been holding a chunk of moldy pipe.

"That'll happen to the best of them," Super said, gesturing at the color.

"What is it?"

"Everything that made him a man."

Super mashed the last of his smoke into the palm of his hand and stuck the butt in his pocket. He got down on his knees and laid a hand on Dinky's brow. My friend's face lay motionless and dull as that of some first-man staring from a wall of ice. When Super rose, two buffalo nickels lay on Dinky's eyes.

"Every man is turned to destruction. And sooner or later every man hears, in his distracted globe, that old voice calling out, *Return, ye children of men, return*."

I remember stumbling over the mannequin and falling to the couch, Dinky's toe an inch away. I remember the crow through the trees, and the sprig in its beak. I remember Basil and Lucille in Super's truck, too weary to care for the monkey on its beads...

We laid Dinky lengthwise, down on the bed of broken dolls. Super hobbled to the cabin, returned with blankets and bags. He kicked his tires, bound with chains, then got behind the wheel. Avey wrapped me in her arm, she took my hand, she kissed me on the cheek. I'd forgotten how good that could be, just a kiss. It was raining again, and somehow I felt free.

IF THERE'S ONE THING I HATE MORE THAN clowns, it's riding in the back of a truck. The last time I'd done that was twenty years past, in Texas, through fields of cotton in the sun, me and my terrier Biscuit watching the dust go swirl, the astonishing skies, the rows of green on either side, fanning to the ends of vision.

Distance will confuse. You were there, and then you weren't. In the moment of sense you make about the difference between the space of then and now, it's all changed, *now* has been snatched away, it's like everything else, an act of colossal dupery, *now* is *then* and *then* a silly idea. There was sense, and there was non-sense, and neither had had any mercy. You think you saw a bird on a post, but the road paid out, and the bird disappeared. There you were trying to puzzle up what little it had shown while sorting through the whim of recent *thens*—what could have been a snake in the road or coil of twine, a man in the shade with a flashlight or hammer or gun—the creature with eyes like topaz, the way they followed you and your dog, wary but detached, its head revolving as you sped by. Then the head shrank, the eyes ebbed to phlegm, to murk, till flatness too had eaten them up, and, again, before you could sort out the mess, it was all just a spot on a line, distressingly significant, distressingly empty, a place holder of sorts for what amounted to yet another of your ideas of the way things are, some hole of wonder in which you could ponder the worth of your mind—did reality need it, did your ego need it, was the thing you'd seen still there once you couldn't see it, did such a matter matter, really, because after all, the way things are has nothing to do with how we think.

A cur bounded up from the ditch, and Biscuit, having flung herself at it, tumbled away in a flurry of dust and hair. It took some time for this to make sense, too. I couldn't say what had happened, even after I'd turned to beat on the cab. My uncle drained his Coors and nudged my toad. He swung to the shoulder and placed his hat and slid from the door and wiped his pants. I shouted what happened, I cried, and back with my dog, I got in the dirt and slobbered on her hair.

"My head's just about as empty as that can there," my uncle said, "but I can tell you now. There ain't but one way to handle a thing like this."

A breeze swept through the fields. The cotton groaned. I never saw him come or go, and yet my uncle stood above me with his gun, his mouth a penciled line. Then my old toad took the gun and ordered me away.

"Leave her," he said, his baldness felloed with light.

"Please, Dad."

"I said leave her."

The shot sounded off before I'd even made the truck. I turned to see my toad with the rifle on his shoulder while behind him my uncle tossed Biscuit in the ditch.

We drove up the road and turned onto another that led to cotton-nowhere. There was a shack with cardboard on the windows and a line strung out with threadbare clothes. An old Studebaker sat by a pump, stuffed full of papers and bottles and gizmos gone bad. Dirty children peered from the door. A man in huaraches and mismatched socks stepped through the kids and spoke to my uncle in Spanish, my uncle replying in pidgin, interrupting his words here and there to spit while waving his hands like his man was a fool. At last he nodded the way we'd come, and the man nodded back. I heard the words *muerto* and *perro* and *well number four.* Then a woman appeared in an oversized tee with a peace sign of red, white, and blue. The man called out to her, then made into the cotton. "*A dónde va?*" said the woman, but the man only raised a hand.

The machinery of hub-bubs and what-nots had started up again, the truck paid out more road. I settled back to silence, never once considering how elemental fear is to the sacred. And Biscuit was there, and then she wasn't. And the sky was blue, and the land was green.

Back home, my uncle gave me a Tootsie Pop, its wrapper with a kid in a headdress shooting an arrow from his bow. When I asked my uncle why he'd killed my dog, he snorted and scratched his nose. "Everthing runs on a leash," he said. "Most especially dogs."

"You don't know anything about dogs."

He tossed back a shot of red eye. "Oh yes I do," he said.

On the farm now, Thomas the Tattooed Whiskey Man is the only guy I really know. In just a few weeks, I told him everything that had happened those days in Tahoe, about me and Avey, and Dinky and Super and Basil and Lucille, everything and the rest. At the part where I'd forgotten the day Biscuit died until I found myself trapped with a dog, a dead man, and a beautiful girl, all in the back of a madman's truck, how my old toad and uncle had shot Biscuit dead without a blink of guilt then tried to buy me off with candy, he said, "And you wonder why I live here on this farm."

We'd been swimming the river in our birthday suits when two of the boss's kids ran off with our threads. They took every stitch, the bananas, and how so full of glee they were. I was about to end the story, lying on the pebbly beach, but mid-sentence Thomas cut me off. He could see how parched I was, he said, which I took to mean he'd decided to show me the still he kept out in the tamarisk, which he then did. We had mason jars to drink the corn, and the kids had left the pouch of smoke. I listened to the water back an angry crow.

"It's quiet here," Thomas said.

"So?"

"So I can hear the noise when it's not."

"That is special, I suppose."

"If it weren't for the quiet, Johnny, there wouldn't be any noise."

That's what they call me here—Johnny. First day I arrived, I had to toil through the rigmarole of how funny it must sound, of how, sure, it was ridiculous and sad as a name could be, but yes, my name was John Henry Doe. They all liked that, and laughed for a beat, but when they tried to break me, I wouldn't say, and couldn't have if I wanted. I'd got too far stuck in my story. The Doe had cut away and John had grown legs. Now it was plain old Johnny.

"How much of this stuff you keep on hand?" I said to Thomas.

"Did you hear what I said?"

"I heard you." I finished rolling his smoke and stood up to leave for another dip, but Thomas held me back.

"All things," he said, "shine brightest in the shadow of what they're not."

"Tell it to the river," I said, and left.

SUPER HAD REACHED THE 50. WE HOVE ON OUT, and in it we were, the midst of cars, an actual line of actual cars, with actual people clutching and banging and shaking actual wheels. This road, too, had been wrecked, though not so badly as up the hill—maintenance crews had cleared the worst. A couple geriatrics in a late model Ford hunkered over the dash behind us, old gramps looking fragile as love, his kisser slack with focus. Horns honked, people screamed, a sheriff flapped his arms. Buildings appeared either side. Through the trees the lake with its little piers and boats swelled against the shore. We passed a shopping center with a supermarket and liquor store and hair salon, a row of commercial atrocities, Dayton's Floors, Fruity's Superior Nails. Farther down, a swampy meadow appeared and then more buildings yet—Douglas County Administrative Offices, the Sheriff and Justice Court. Some hokey chapel floated past, up on a hillock, the kind of hole where you slap on a tux before marriage to a song by Elvis.

We hove on. A golf course swam by, the polders flooded out, the lake out past it again. Then came the casinos, looming like teeth, Caesar's here, Horizon there, and Bill's and Harvey's and Harrah's. People were still rushing in and out with coin buckets for the slots. By their faces, they could've been on Dagobah and never known, some bright with fever, others in its wake so grim. That the world was breaking to pieces didn't mean poodly lark.

But we hove on. Nevada became California. Past pizza joints and past motels we chugged and choked, past tourist traps and pharmacies and jewelers and boutiques, here a grocer, there a cleaner, here a seller of knives and guns. A McDonald's sailed by, then a diner, then a bodega for cigarettes and gas. The world flowed away in a psychedelic stream of greens and greys, a volte-face of perception. We came to a stretch of cars like monsters drowned, submerged in water to their roofs. Steam drifted from them, exhaust through the water, on one a family—mommy and daddy and their whey-faced runts—heavy with hopelessness and wear. Later, three children cried in a boat, pushed by a man in slickers, the water to his thighs.

At the river, the bridge poured out like a floating road. Trucks in water wheels-high made giant wakes, their beds crammed with chattel and children and pets. Engines coughed and rain thrummed and ceased and thrummed again. Near the Long's Drugs, the parking lot had flooded to the storefront itself. Government vehicles loaded with sandbags moved to and fro, but we didn't stop, but hove on through. Finally a red and white billboard pointed the way to Barton Memorial Hospital. We turned down a road with a trailer park and tenements, and suddenly we were there.

The hospital reminded me of some resort-asylum for rich drunks and addicts. A porte-cochère with a river-rock facade and clear-pine trim presided over the roundabout. On either side the bureaucrats had planted boxy lawns studded with ornamental plums and jeffrey pines, and flowerbeds full of bark.

Super stepped from the truck and mumbled to his dog, then Basil hobbled out, *sans* Lucille.

"Now here's a rumbling bellyful," the old man said, raking at his beard. "Here's lunatics and rage."

Basil squinted. He ran a hand across his face and hawked out a loogie. He was beat to shit. "I still can't tell," he said, and his voice sounded worse than he looked, "if this guy's the devil or a nine-to-five fool." He stooped for the lighter he'd dropped. "I'm dying here."

"Most times it's the fool's the prophet," Super said, and tickled Basil's chin.

"Show me the profit here, and I'll cut off my right hand." Basil was turning in a slow circle, now, his arms spread wide.

"Maybe," Avey said, "you should wait for us to bring you a wheelchair."

"Ha," Basil said.

"They'll bandage up your dogs," I said. "They might even help you walk."

Super dropped the tailgate and took up Dinky's feet. A portly man with a goose down parka and pipe in his mouth glanced our way, a paper at his bald spot. It seemed he'd keep on, but then he fixed on our friend with the dolls. "Hope that's not what I think it is," he said, and stopped to light the pipe.

"Beat it, yuppie," Basil said.

"Let's get, Horatio."

"Basil's right, Super," Avey said. "It's probably not the best idea to go traipsing in there with a… with Dinky like he is."

"That's true," I said.

"Oh will you now."

Avey locked eyes with Super. "This is no time for screwing around," she said, somehow effectively. For once the old man was silent.

"Let's just go in there and see what they want," Basil said.

"They'll call the cops on us, I bet," I said, thinking as I did how much Basil hated humans in a uniform, but most especially cops.

"They'll take one look at Dinky and know it was an accident."

"It's no use standing here guessing," I said.

Basil raised an arm that I slid under, Avey did, too, and off we went.

The triage windows were jammed. Before one sat a father with his teenage son, his ankle in a cast of rags. Around the other, an entire family had clustered, all of them jabbering one atop the other in a blur of non-Mexican Spanish. The place stunk of armpits, blood, carpet cleaner, dust. Everywhere people were roiling in fits, and those who weren't looked on the verge. When finally the kid with the ankle got up, I slid into the seat before some bleeding woman and told her it was life and death.

"But you can't do that," she said. She dropped her rotten tissue on the counter and tapped at the window to the nurse behind it. "Tell him he can't do that," she said.

"You can't do that," said the nurse. She was young and appallingly thin, with close-set eyes and enormous specs.

"I'm a hemophiliac," said the woman. "You just can't do that."

I leaned into the speaker and told the nurse, "My friend is dead."

"This is very important, miss," the hemophiliac said. "Would you please tell him he just can't do that?"

"Where is this friend?" said the nurse, whose name by her tag was "Wendy."

"In the back of our truck."

"And you're sure he's deceased."

"Listen, miss," Basil said, "no disrespect intended, but we're in no mood for snazzy gags. You got a stretcher or something we can haul him in on?"

Wendy shot Basil a smile meant to wither.

"He's got problems, too," I said.

"What's wrong with him."

"His feet." I pointed at Basil's feet. "What's your procedure for taking in, you know, for taking in corpses?"

Wendy saw that we weren't joking. She slid her pen into the board with the sign-in list. The hemophiliac had started harping again, but Wendy stifled her with a hand. "We'll have some nurses come out with a gurney," she told me, her voice gone mellow. "They'll have to admit the body through the ambulance bay."

"Here's my number," I said, "and this is his license. How long you think they'll be?"

"I'll be right back," she said.

Rockets would sigh that night, high over this somber town. They'd explode in the clouds and mingle the rain of that outcry with the rain that had been and would be, and though that show might gesture toward elegance, even toward a grotesque munificence, it would never quite make the grade. How is it we think that to achieve ourselves we must stand on the backs of notions? Let's bring the stars down to earth. Let's cut down a tree to hang the stars on. Let's maim our blunders with time, and with whispers and gifts and cheap perfume. In the crowd we'll savor the taste of false vitality and pretend we're not ourselves, not even people, but only an image of the sights around. Orgy of the whir, orgy of the hum, in these we'll search for the things we'd been told we could hope to be. Behind the smile on that man, the gaze of that girl—there's but an effigy, the shimmer of so many days pushed through—ching-a-ling-ching, rattle-bang-boom: shriek, laugh, cry, groan. There on the streets, in the swarming casinos, we'd watch the past slide off and wait for the bells to toll a new year. Who knows what it means to police their days? This night we'd need to shrink the field, lower the boom, raise high the lanterns, red and green and gold. And the meager light we'd thought we made for ourselves would be little more than the twilight we thought we knew. The rockets would care for the rest. They'd explode, and we would sigh, and the faces around us, whatever they might be, would give comfort, if only by their numbers. Because tomorrow would be new, a brand new month and year. Let the night take our money and our pain. Yes, and yes. Calendar on…

Later, smiling at Basil and Lucille as they danced among the crowds, the old man would say, "It's survival of the slickest, boy, and that's something even the blind can see." And then he'd turn away, his face a puzzle, mumbling about maltworms and knaves, and vanish in the people, Fortinbras at his heel. I thought of Joubert's notion of the nest in the mind of the bird. All over the world, this very moment even, creatures were busy building homes—nests and hives and caves and dens and tunnels and lairs and dams, and hobo jungles and tenement slums, and birdhouses, and dovecotes, and dumps—everywhere, everywhere, a place for each and all. That's why we could play tonight, and that's why we could pray tomorrow. You want your moments, you need a place to make them, the way you need that place to remember and regret. We'd need roofs over our heads when it was said and done, and pillows beneath them, else how could we trick ourselves for even a moment with the platitudes that help to make us real? I'm as good as gold, and you're an angel in disguise, and the devil may care, though not, perhaps, until tomorrow, so hey, run with the money while you can, baby, run, you're a nine days' wonder… God is not just one. Our clichés tell us so every minute.

Wendy never returned. How could I hope to know what would be? I took Avey's hand, and we turned to face the crowd. A series of watercolors lined the walls, made by kids. Most scenes were happy families, father on the left, the tallest, followed by mom and the children by height, with a dog at the end: Daddy, Mommy, Stephanie, Abbie, Socks. There was a drawing too of a gold-haired woman with a jagged smile and flat blue eyes. That was it—no father, no children, no dog. Beneath her, in lopsided scrawl, was the single word, MOM. And mom was crying, and her tears were blood. Barry Manilow muzak piped through the speakers, just below the general din, "Copacabana," it seemed, though I didn't know for sure. Next to a TV running a soap sat a hundred gallon aquarium, filled, like the room its people, with all manner of fish. I watched them bump through a maze of shipwrecks and logs, endlessly gaping, until an old coot hobbled by, stinking of baby food and bad cologne, and a little girl maybe four years old let out a howl only children can make, packed with the world's own pain and sin. At that, her mother jerked her wrist and quick as light snatched the slipper from her foot and rapped the child's head. And then a woman was at my ear, with braces on her teeth and Mary Hartman braids.

"He's outside," Avey told her.

"In the parking lot?" said the woman's colleague. Stocky like a miner, she had a mullet with gelled spikes on top and a stringy mane down her back—the kind of do middle-aged lesbians have been rocking for a decade or so.

"In our truck," said Basil. He'd limped over once he realized the women had come for us. "You guys're going to take him?"

The stocky woman clasped her hands at her waist and wore a face reminiscent of certain preschool teachers, deceptively bemused, falsely sympathetic. "Do you know what happened?" she said.

"We had an accident," I said.

"An accident," said the tall gal. Now she was the sweet one. No crappy faces or half-baked pity. She was for real.

"We had a wreck last night."

"Up on the mountain," Basil said.

"And then what," said the stocky one, crossing her arms.

"They went out for some ice," Avey said, "and got into a wreck. When we woke up this morning he'd… you know." She started for the door. "You'll probably want to see for yourselves."

"You got something to carry him in on?" Basil said.

The stocky woman twirled the tail at her shoulder. "I'm going to pack it over my shoulder," she said.

"Pardon?" Basil said.

"I'm exceptionally well conditioned," the woman said.

"Come on, Karen," said the tall one with a big metal smile. She was a peach, this gal, for real. I guessed she had a houseful of animals, not cats, but dogs. "Eden," said her tag.

Basil had already made it to the first set of sliding doors. "When you're finished, maybe you could take care of him, too," I said. "I know you're busy and all."

"What's your name?"

It occurred to me that in my polka dot shirt and muddy boots I was still dressed like a clown. "He's in pretty bad shape, you know."

"Maybe we should have a look at you first," Eden said.

With her gurney on wheels, Nurse Karen marched out and fell in beside us. Super had enfolded Lucille with an arm to mumble his wisdom as she cried, and she had let him do it. The tailgate was open still, Dinky exposed to all who cared. Once again it began to rain.

"What're you doing?" Lucille said, her face wide with horror. Nurse Karen had hopped up and crouched near Dinky's head.

"Now, now," said the old man.

"Mind if we take it with the blanket?"

"*It?*" Lucille said.

Super peeled off from Lucille to face Nurse Karen. "You'll excuse our saying so, misses, but we'll have to ask you to disembark the wheels till we've given the boy his due."

"Looks like a three-phase operation," Nurse Karen said to Eden. "Slide it down—"

"Step off the wheels, misses," Super said, "if you please."

Nurse Karen's face hardened. "As you can see, sir, we're much too busy for formalities. Just take up the feet," she said to Eden, "and slide it down far enough for us to make the turn."

"That's it?" Lucille said. "You're just going to haul him away?"

"Maybe you could give us a minute?" I said to Eden.

"Karen?" she said.

Nurse Karen bounced from the truck and began to pace.

"It's raining," Eden said to me. "So..."

"Thanks," said Avey.

Super drew off the blanket... Birds were in the trees... I smelled ice cream, I smelled rain... In the distance I heard laughter, but knew it wouldn't count—no one counts laughter, because laughter disappears... I was just an animal, words on the lake... Then a bird flew, and the rest flew after, and Basil limped up and took Dinky's feet and pulled his shoulders to the gate, where Super spun him even to it—our old pal Dinky, he was dead.

I hadn't seen the geeze take his nickels from Dinky's eyes, but somehow he had, only to lay them down again and step back cap in hand.

"It is clear, friends," he said, his voice grown solemn, "that before us lies a perturbed spirit without a finger on his lips to smother grief. It's our job to send him off with nary a whisper at his ears, though he be alone. Blood or no blood, you were his brothers and sisters. And so you loved the boy as we did. You don't have to croak for us to see how forty thousand brigands couldn't add to our sum, not with all their stolen love. For ourselves, we'd eat a crocodile if it meant he'd be delivered, ready to bend and give and move through the world with a smile. And we know you'd do it, too. Give this boy his due, friends, then cut the line with hearts full of thanks and cheer."

Some gawkers had massed about twenty feet off. Lucille was shuddering, she was crying so hard. She took Dinky's hand and kissed and pressed it to her cheek. Then she lurched into the truck.

"What the fuck're you staring at?" Basil said to the gawkers. It wasn't until he'd started toward them that they began to part. A woman walked by, shielding her daughter's eyes.

"But what is it, Mommy?" the child said.

"That's right," Basil said. "Scram!"

"Finished?" said Nurse Karen.

I touched Dinky's hand. A crust of blood had grown along the top of one of his nails. Avey held me. Her face was swollen.

"Take him," she said.

"Wait," Basil said. He brought out a guitar pick—Paul Stanley's, I knew—and tucked it into Dinky's shirt. "Rock and roll, buddy," he said. "We'll catch you on the rebound."

And that was it. No police, no questions, no forms. Nurse Karen and Eden just put our pal on the gurney and whisked him through the doors. Poof! He was there, and then he wasn't. Disgusting. Tremendous. Done.

Super's dolls covered the bed of his truck, plastic eyes rolling, plastic hair clinging to horrible plastic heads. No sign of sun, no sign of shit but *mucho* rain and *mucho* mud. A wind rose up and drove the trees…

Times like this the whole blasted planet creaks on its hinges, waiting for you to give, the way it knows you will, if you're ordinary… Your life's just residue. You're the sloughing-offs of so many sloughing-offs you couldn't say which was which or what went where and when. You can't see between the main or remains anymore, the remains or the remainder's residue. All you know is flux and everflux, the monstrous process—in the big sense, the really big sense—of eating and shitting and eating and shitting and eating… For a single hideous moment, there in the slippery rain, surrounded by the only people I'd ever truly known and who for that reason were strangers, I saw the ruin of distinctions. The weight of Dinky's absence became the weight of Dinky's presence. His death had become his life, his laughter my memory of it, my memory the laughing world's. Beauty and terror, the sacred and the feared—these had lost their color…

"You want me to get in the back a while?" Basil said, his eyes gone crooked the way they did when he grew tired.

"Might as well take care of your feet while we're here," I said.

"Yeah," Avey said. "You wait much longer, and they might have to amputate."

"Go on, boy," said the geeze. "That old gal with the tracks in her mouth'll take good care."

Basil limped to his girl, who hadn't seemed so much as to blink. "You okay?" He took her hand, but she didn't twitch. "I'll be back in a flash with a Coke on ice," he said, "just the way you like it."

IT WASN'T TILL LATER, AS WE LAY IN OUR MOTEL, that Avey said why she told Lucille what she told her while Basil fixed his feet.

"I'm never going to see those people again," Avey said from her pillow.

"How do you figure?"

"You think this is the first time I've hit a snag?"

"How aren't you going to see them?"

"You won't either."

"Avey," I said. "They're all I've got."

She ran a finger down my chest. She kissed me there, she kissed my mouth. "*Were*, baby," she said, "and *had*." I considered the stains on the ceiling, adjusting to her words. "You know it's over," she said. "I saw it coming a week after I met you guys, and I'm slow."

"That still doesn't say why you had to tell her all that."

"It made her feel better."

"But it's just a name."

"A name is not a name is not a name. And it sure as hell isn't *me*."

I waited for her to continue, but she rolled to her back and took my hand and smiled.

"That's fucked up," I said.

“Yeah?”

“Look. I know you’re restless. What I don’t get is, why me?”

“A long time ago,” she said, “just after I’d run away from home the first time, I bought a fifty-cent box of chow mein down on 42nd street, in New York. I ate it all, and when I finished, I ate the fortune cookie, too. You want to know what the fortune said?”

“Fortune’s are for weaklings,” I said.

“It said, *Discontent is the first step in the progress of a man or a nation.*”

I didn’t have to tell her the idea was worth regard. But neither did I want to say something too glib or hifalutin.

“Traveling cures these things,” she said. “I’m on the road. My secrets are my steps.”

“Sounds like a fancy way to say you’re just a liar.”

“Let’s go to sleep.”

“If it’s the way you say it is, then why didn’t you tell her your name was Mud?”

Avey put two fingers on my lips. “I’ve never told anybody that,” she said. “Not even you.”

There must’ve been more to Avey’s telling Lucille her real name than she’d admit. Our friend had died, the woman was filled with grief. Lucille wouldn’t’ve cared if Avey had said her name was Trash.

It was hard at first. Lucille’s silence, it seemed, was a forest through which she couldn’t find her way. We asked how she felt, for nothing. We asked was she tired, the same. We asked what she wanted now we were free, but still she said not a word. I flicked the monkey so it bumped and spun.

“The old man calls this thing José,” I said. “As if at any minute it might want to rhumba.”

Lucille was listening now. Her eyes had kicked the blur. She even almost laughed, I thought.

"I notice you haven't called me Elmira," Avey said.

"I like Hickory better."

"What if I told you Elmira's no more my name than Hickory?"

"I'd say that was a good thing."

"What if I told you it's Avey?"

"You want to be called Avey, I'll call you Avey. You want the other, I'll call you that. Just tell me what you want."

"I want for you to be happy."

"Basil wants to get his truck," said Lucille.

The old man had remained quiet in the drizzle. "What about him?" Avey said.

"He needs us right now," I said.

"Somebody needs somebody," Lucille said.

"The man is back in town!"

And so he was: Basil Badalamente, musician, doofus, drunk, asshole-cum-friend, friend-cum-foe, and foe-champ, all in the sense of huge, of extraordinaire, of bigger than life itself. Yes, yes, yes, Basil was big, Basil was huge, as huge as ever and maybe huger, but that didn't mean he wasn't a fake. Fakes was what we were, really, every last one of us, and fakery was our game, especially times like these. There's no such thing, after all, as the Comedown, so long as we never called it. Ergo, with fakery and lies, this had become routine. *I am not ugly, but stoked. I am not wounded, but charmed. I am not hurt, but pissed. And I will laugh at it all—ha! ha!—and keep on laughing—ha! ha! ha!—down to the putrid dregs.* Basil, undisputed King of the Fakes, now threw down his cane and proffered a Coke on ice.

"Am I good, baby," he said, "or am I *good*?"

I took the soda. "Mighty white of you, friend."

"How are you?" Lucille said.

He looked like a hairy scab. But to see his twinkling eyes and mouthful of teeth, you'd think he thought himself a hawk. "On top of the world," he said. "On top of the freaking world!"

"Hey, Super," Avey said, tugging at the old man's sleeve. "You ready?"

"Our name's Steady," Super said.

"We thought we'd pick up some clothes," I told Basil, "then hit a motel and place to eat. Then you can see about the Cruiser."

"That okay with you, geeze?" Basil said to Super.

"So long as Horatio here lives to tell the tale, we can run the race." And at that, Fortinbras the dog appeared in the bed behind his master.

"We're not getting back there again," I said.

Lucille sat up to protest, but Avey cut her off. "And we shant be drawing straws."

"It's only just down the way," Basil said.

I offered Lucille the Coke. Little by little her face grew soft. "I'm sorry," she said at last.

We didn't say a word. There was no word to say. Her sorrow, I saw, was more than she herself could say. Her face was the saying, and the wet of her eye. I thought of infants and of hatchlings, and of the trillions of creatures searching through this world, those in this land of wintry muck and those out there, beneath the sun, away at the world's ends. Lucille was in her hair shirt. Times like this you don't say dook. What you do is breathe.

Super drew the door and stepped aside. "Well sure you are," he said. "Sorrow's *always* better than laughter." Avey got out, then Lucille, the old man tapped his chest and grinned. "It's by sadness the heart's made good."

"If only this were another day," Lucille said.

"Oh, but you're wrong, young misses. This here day's better than the rest, by far."

"Not to change the subject or anything," Avey said, "but do you know where these guys can get a change of clothes for cheap?"

Super said he did, and sure enough, at the 89 and 50, it was: a Millers Outpost, like a beacon from the mist. With the $52.38 in my pocket, the bills completely soaked, I bought some 501s, a cheap blue flannel and long sleeve tee, and was left with some change till I could tap my nest egg, 262 lousy bucks. Basil got identical stuff, fifty sizes larger, and a pair of Reeboks, size 17, for the bindings on his feet.

"You wouldn't happen to have a paper I could buy?" I said to the kid who helped us. He was a white boy, skinny as Fred Astaire, with a baseball cap and little bald head and giant shirt across which, in skate-punk graffiti, read the word *THINK!*

"Don't be crazy, man." He took a paper from under the reg and tossed it on the counter. "Y'all can *have* it."

"Slap me some skin," I said, and held out my hand.

The kid eyed my hand like it might become a snake. "You a weird-ass."

"Slap me some skin," I said.

Basil was waiting. The kid ran his hand across mine, way too fast, and our business was complete. "You a weird-ass dude," he said. "I check you out."

I opened the paper. LAKE MAROONED BY TORRENTIAL RAIN, said the headline. Basil leaned over my shoulder:

*With rushing floodwaters undermining U.S. Highway 50 in numerous locations, the main route from Sacramento to South Lake Tahoe will remain closed indefinitely… Rain and melting snow have filled rivers and caused dangerous mudslides throughout the Tahoe Basin, where more than 2,000 US West customers were without phone service… About 7,300 Northern California customers were without power yesterday, while about*

*13,000 Washington households were without power, down from a peak of 250,000…*

"I wasn't going anywhere, anyway," Basil said. "You going anywhere?"

"I'm just a weird-ass, Basil. You know?"

He pinched one of his little ears, and it struck me he didn't have his hat. He'd slept and showered and shit with the thing for the better part of ten forsaken years, and now, someway, it was lost.

"Speaking for myself," he said, "I'm one famished son of a bitch."

"We need a room," I said.

"Mark my words. We'll be sleeping in the old man's crate."

On top of the flooding, it was New Year's Eve, a not-so-small fact that happened to've slipped my mind. Super rolled to the 50 again and headed for Nevada. The world was still a sad-sack place, its folks a sad-sack lot. Every roach trap along the way had someone sleeping in a closet. Maybe he was right, Basil, and we were doomed to a night in the basement of a church, eating macaroons and Jello with bluehairs and bums and other sundry dopes.

Through this spot and that we made our way, past the unlucky bastards we'd seen the journey in, the roofs of their cars nearly swallowed. A grown man sat on one, a big old dude with a Grizzly Adams beard and shearling vest. From a distance it seemed he was talking to himself, or maybe even singing, but closer it grew plain the bear was sobbing like a kitten. He just stood there on display, right in the open, pouring out his guts.

"Pity," Super said, "never cries in the streets. But wisdom. Every day it's howling on the roads, and not a varlet hears it."

Was he a cream puff, this man? We thought not, though, again, he was no insensitive beast… The song about the man who couldn't cry until he'd been taken to the place for the insensitive and insane. Who after that not only cried, but cried every time it rained. Who once it had rained for forty days and forty nights died on the forty-first day—he just dehydrated and died…

And it was true, I thought: he was there, and then he wasn't…

We hove on, getting the brush at every joint—stuck in and shut out, all at once. I picked up the paper. "'Fed by a week of pounding rain and melting snow,'" I read, "'Lake Tahoe rose to its highest level in modern times Tuesday, rising six inches in a day to surpass the lake's legal storage capacity—'"

"Needles in your brain, Horatio, is all that is."

"Says here it's a twelve hour drive just to Sacramento."

"We got a friend," Super said. "Up yonder."

"What friend is that," Avey said.

"Fear not, butterfly. She will feed you."

Around the bend the lake rolled into view once more, turbulent, vast, and blue, roiling with whitecaps, and scarves of mist, and not a single squawking gull, nothing from a painting on a doctor's wall, just apathy, brutal, just eternity, cruel. A flooded shopping center drifted past, and then a golf course, flooded, too. Then more concerns, the Mickey D's again, the crowded Shell's, that diner packed with refugees and locals and archangels and creeps. And then we were parked before the Thunder Chief Motel, a drowsy looking joint with dripping eaves and needles on the porch. But just like the rest, this one had its blinking sign: NO VACANCY.

"I know you can read," I told the old man.

"We've got a friend."

"By the looks of it," Avey said, "he's doing a good business."

The old man wriggled in his seat. I looked at his fingers on the wheel: BEND and GIVE.

"What's the deal?" Basil said.

"The old man says he's got a friend in there," Avey said.

"The implication," I said, "is he can somehow squeeze us in."

"I'll hold my breath," Basil said.

Inside, I rang the bell. To the left hung a pic of two of the scariest entities I had ever seen. The woman reminded me of something from Poe, risen from ancestral vaults. She had a forehead like a boxing glove, her eyes bulged over a steak-knife nose above a scratch for lips, and her beehive do was purple. Next to her, and much taller, stood her giant of a freak, Herman Munster's brother, his iron hair in a bowl-cut and skin like the rinds on nasty cheese. At least the office was warm. It smelled of TV dinners and mentholated smoke. I rang the bell again.

"Be right with you," said a voice from behind a half-drawn door.

I had my arm around Avey. She looked at me and smiled. I wanted to be alone with her, in the warmth of a room with chocolate and toast, beneath some grandma's quilt. We'd murmur to each other, we'd sleep, I'd rest in the belly of her sighs. I wanted to say, *I love you*, but mumbled, "Take your time."

The guy through the door was the monster in the pic, the selfsame bizzaro of a guy. He was not, however, clad in a tux, but bicycling shorts and a pale green tee that said MARINE WORLD, AFRICA USA. He was barefoot. Most of his toenails were black. Best of all, he was an inch or two taller than Basil, pushing seven feet.

"What can we do for you kids?" he said, and placed a dish of olives on the counter.

It took me a second to find my voice. "Hows about telling us you accidentally switched on your NO VACANCY sign?"

"Since Moses got the tablets," said the man, "I been sitting in this office. That's a long time, you know." I picked up a postcard featuring a Fabio-type lunk in a g-string, smoldering with his pinched blue eyes and ridiculous bulge. It said FABULOUS LAKE TAHOE. "And in all that time," the man said, "I haven't seen anything like what we've got going on here." Now that he'd moved closer, the sacks beneath eyes took on a whole new meaning. "I ask you," he said, "would either one of you kids go out in this if you did not absolutely have to?"

"So you did make a mistake with the sign," Avey said.

The man smacked his lips. "Nincompoops I think the world is spawning these days," he said. "If you ask me, that's what I'd say. This genius of a couple, it turns out, decided they were going to try to make it home tonight. Only fifteen minutes ago they conceived of this exploit."

"You're kidding," I said.

The man crammed a handful of olives in his mouth. "Do I look like the kind who kids?"

"Depends on what the-kind-who-kids looks like," I said.

The man took a step back from the counter and held out his arms. "The father of our country?" he said, smacking on his olives. "He's a big fat nothing next to me."

"How much," Avey said.

"Maybe I'm wrong, I don't know. But I think you'll agree that $59.95, plus tax, is a precious good deal."

"We'll take it."

"Just the two of you?"

"We've got three more outside."

"Not to be slippery, but that will make it $89.95." From behind a pair of thrift store specs, he took up a pencil and licked its tip. "Two king-sizes ought to keep you, I think."

"You know an old man named Super?" Avey said.

"That I cannot say."

"He says he knows you."

"Lots of people say they know me when I don't know them from Jehoshaphat."

"He's right outside." I pointed out the window, but go figure, Super had disappeared. "Well," I said, "he was a minute ago."

"He couldn't've gone far," said the man. He slid his check-in book my way. "Now if one of you gentle people would be so kind as to share your intimates." He snuck another peep outside. "You may think I'm plotzing, but my eyes, they tell me there's a little monkey out there, dangling in that truck, I swear."

"Plotzing you are not," Avey said.

The man shook his head. "Then I wasn't plotzing."

I asked Basil to cover the tab till we could reach a bank.

"You got dough in the bank?" he said. I looked at him. A wad of bills appeared in his hand. "Here."

The room was typical, a tube on the wall, plastic drinking cups and cheap white towels, the Hallmark photo of two owls in a hole in a tree. Lucille wanted to get in bed but Basil wouldn't let her. He needed her to get his truck. Triple A told us such conditions would usually keep us waiting two or three hours, but it just so happened a man was nearby. Fifteen minutes later, our buddies were gone.

Not until the door had shut behind them and the hush came down did I comprehend: this was the real world, this normality, we were safe again in the real world now, Avey and I were alone.

Her eyes were black, her skin a lake of shadows and cream. A thick green light had fallen on her, full of swirling motes. Her mouth, her lips, her teeth—she was all too terribly edible, so deceptive, so pure.

I imagined her finger along my teeth and over my tongue, and then another finger and another until soon her hand had eased down my throat, and then her arm, too, and other hand

and arm, and her face, and head, and on, till she was all inside. I touched her mouth. Her eyelids drooped.

"So pretty," I said.

She blushed. "Really?"

I plucked her nose and stuck my thumb between my fingers. "Really."

Avey kissed me again, and we laughed.

"I like you, AJ," she said.

"I like you, Mud."

It was unbelievably quiet. Everything lay quiet, everything still. The room was a cave under water and all that was in it a merking's things, silent as the depths, lovely and green, a silence only the gifted could know, the gifted and the drowned. Avey sat on my lap.

"I feel so greasy," she said.

I put my face in her neck, her hair. We rocked to and fro. Such stillness, such quiet, what a world...

And the rain kept raining, down the mountains, into rivers and lakes...

"Speaking of which," she said at last, "did you know there was some greasy spoon down the way?"

"I saw it."

"Let's walk down there."

"What about Super?"

"You really like that old guy, don't you."

"He's the kind of guy who scares you while he makes you laugh. But I feel sorry for him. I don't know why."

"He's a lonely man."

"His truck's outside."

"Come on."

"I don't want to be anything like him," I said. Avey shook

her head. "But then again, I want to be exactly like him." Avey smiled. "You miss Dinky?"

"I started missing Dinky the day we met."

"It's like he's on vacation," I said. "Like he left on a train."

"Come on."

I took her hand. "I like you, Mud."

Again she smiled. "I can see that, AJ. I like you, too."

A DARK-SKINNED MAN WITH KRIS KRINGLE EYES and big gold teeth met us at the door and took our name.

"Is cold out there," he said, "and warm in here. We take good care of you."

Here was a place full of people who might never have known they were trapped in a storm. Families of all sorts had jammed the room to the gunnels. Maple syrup and waffles, hash browns and crepes, and pork chops and ketchup and muffins and toast, and burgers, too, and corned beef and sauerkraut on rye, and hot chocolate and tea, and onions and root beer and coffee and milk, and French toast, and raspberry jam. Smells swirled round us thick with the hum of satisfied speech, a great single body of glistening eyes and munching mouths, the clatter and clink of spoons in cups and forks on plates, and the steamy hiss of fryer and grill, and the banter of waitresses, children, cooks. An infant sat in her mother's lap, feeding from a bottle. The mother herself was engaged in talk with a boy in a mask, waving a plastic gun, another, I guessed, of her many. The boy had asked about the difference between bacon and ham, whereon she took the baby's foot and jiggled its toes. "This little piggy," she said, "went to the market. This little piggy stayed home…" The boy tore off his mask and squealed. "Oink, oink!" he shouted. "Oink!" Two girls maybe seven or eight were playing a game of patty cakes.

An old woman sat with her old man holding hands in silence, not for nothing to say, I could see, but for the glow that was The Real. Red and green crepe bunting festooned the place. Lights twinkled, music purred.

A woman approached. She was pregnant and wore her hair in a braid, tied up top with a bow of white taffeta. Around her neck on a silver chain hung a silver ball that tinkled as she moved. She was tall and thin, and her eyes gleamed with such joy, I had never seen. I recognized the song, by Captain & Tennille—*I will! I will! I will!*

"Hello, hello," the woman said. I wanted to call her Old Lady Pear, but she wasn't old, but like a pear. "I sure do hope you two are ready to eat, because we're ready to serve you. Ready spaghetti!"

"I am no lie, eh?" said the man with gold teeth as the woman led us off.

"What's your name?" Avey said.

"My name," said the woman, and pinched the chain above her silver ball, "is Robin. Did I sprinkle magic dust on you yet?"

"I don't think we've had the pleasure," I said.

"Never say never," she said, and giggled. She leaned first to Avey's side of the booth and then to mine and shook the ball so it tinkled. "All of us girls have them," she said. "I was the first. Now every girl gets one on her birthday. We're all fairy sisters!"

"You're lucky," Avey said.

"You don't know the *half* of it," Robin said. She stood back and gleamed. "You two look like you could use a good strong cup of motor starter!"

"Is she cool or what?" Avey said when Robin had left.

"Straight from a book," I said.

Robin came back with coffee and filled our cups. It was so

hot and black and the steam so thick I almost didn't want to drink it. Nothing, it seemed, had been so inviting for years.

"I've told you my name," said Robin, "but you haven't told me yours."

"I'm Avey. That's AJ."

"Well, Avey and AJ, would you mind if I make a suggestion?"

"I don't know…" Avey said, drawing out the words.

"*Swiss Boysenberry Crepes.*"

"You like those, do you?"

"Like them?" Robin wore heavy blue eye shadow that glistened when she blinked. "Goodness, AJ. I could eat those until they came out my ears!"

"Well what are you waiting for?" I said. "This guy's starving."

Robin's smile never left. Avey touched her arm. "Don't take it personally, but I'm kind of in the mood for eggs."

"I do love eggs," said Robin as her hand described a circle round her belly. "They make me think of how fast my little one here's gone from being a little teensy egg to *this*."

"When're you due?" I said.

"Make me a promise?" Robin said.

"Depends."

Robin giggled. "Think of me on Ground Hog Day!" she said, somehow able to laugh and talk at once.

"That's it?" I said. "The big day?"

"The big day. Pop!" Robin poked her belly. "Now about those eggs," she said. "We can make them any way you like, scrambled hard or soft, soft boiled, hard boiled, poached, sunnyside-up, over easy, over hard, what's your pleasure, Avey? Speak now or I'll have to come again!"

"Scrambled," Avey said, "with cheese. And toast and hash browns and jelly. And orange juice, too. Doesn't orange juice sound divine?" she said.

"Orange juice sounds just lovely," I said.

"I can't believe how perfect you two are," Robin said. "It makes me all warm and mushy inside just to see you. How long have you been married?"

"We're not," Avey said.

"Well you should be," Robin said. She spun round on her pediatric shoes and shouted. "Yoo-*hoo*, Ma-*ri*-a!" A curvy girl with kinky hair and tiny teeth pattered to the table. "Do they or do they not look like the *per*fect couple?"

Robin hadn't lied about the silver balls. Maria pulled one from her blouse and shook it. "It's your destiny," she said.

"See?" Robin said.

"You're a regular gypsy," I said.

"I'm good, I'm bad," Robin said, "though I might be a little ugly."

"*No*," Avey said.

"Yes!" One of the cooks called Robin's name, and she jumped. "Goodness. They'll have my head on a platter before I know it. I've got to get your order filled."

The place was really bustling, the air enough to swoon. Waitresses worked their way through the aisles, each with a silver ball on a silver chain. Two construction-type guys sat hunkered over plates full of biscuits and gravy and pancakes and butter and bacon, all good things for hungry working men. Young and upcoming professionals decked out in Calvin Klein shades and Gucci skiwear clambered round tables loaded with grub, grandmas and grandpas, as well, gnawing on bones and sucking down fries, their grandsons and -daughters righteously porking along. Here was the ontology of oneness in a world gone mad, the music of chaos and bliss, some bright and risen band of lovelies playing for our ears only. Or maybe it was the way things had been and would always be, plain as a mountain, jeering at my stupor with good-natured amplitude until finally, like a man who'd been anesthetized, like it knew would be, I came round. The fragrance of so many meals, and the gorgeous din, the coffee in my mouth, hot with sugar and cream, these were a euphony all their own. Since I could remember, this was the first time my body had keened with a sense the world calls delight. My head swam loud with textures, tastes, colors, sound. On every wall hung pictures of the famous who'd graced the joint, a regular Vegas pantheon. There was Crystal Gayle in a white lace dress, and The Oak Ridge Boys with pompadours and smiles, the Denvers, too, John and Bob, and Wayne Newton, and Sammy Davis Jr, and Three Dog Night. The cheese factor was as high as the spirits. Hosannas from the sky couldn't have sweetened the pot.

"Avey," I said. She didn't answer. She only looked. "I don't know," I said. "It's like this place fills me with a huge sense of, I don't know, well-being, I guess."

"That is *so* weird," Avey said like a high school bimbo, though I loved her for it anyway, "because that's exactly how I feel, too."

"It's a Brady Bunch thing," I said.

"I wish I could live here."

"Me, too," I said. "With you."

"Really?"

"Really."

"Me, I mean, with you."

Steam like genies swarmed from our plates when Robin set them down, boysenberries oozed across my crepes, cheese over Avey's eggs, them and mounds of butter. A smorgasbord of syrup magically appeared—strawberry, raspberry, blueberry, maple—the whole goddamned works. And though I'd never asked, Robin had brought me a giant glass of milk. If Avey's face was a picture of mine, we must have looked the King and Queen of Earth.

"Say, Robin."

"Yes, dear?"

"You wouldn't by any chance know a silver-haired man called Super?"

"Super Duper? Supercalifragilisticexpialidocious?"

"Yeah, yeah," I said. "You know him?"

"Can't say I do."

"You've heard of him then," Avey said.

"Nope."

"Then how'd you know his name?"

"Silly! Everyone is super-duper to me!"

Avey and I laid into our meals. For a solid five minutes we didn't say a word. Finally I looked up. Avey was staring with a smile.

"What?" I said, looking at my shirt to see if I'd drooled. "Do I have a bat in the cave or what?"

"Can't a girl just smile?"

I took Avey's hands. I leaned across the table and kissed her. "Marry me," I said. "Today. Right now."

"AJ."

"Marry me. We can go into Nevada and get hitched today. It's no secret the way I feel about you. Besides, you heard what that woman said."

"That they're fairies?"

"That it's in the stars, you. Marry me."

Avey took a sip of water. She leaned into her seat. "*AaaaaaJaaaaay.*"

"AJ nothing. Let's do it."

My girl was smiling, the way humans do when the world turns strange, my girl was stirring her eggs. I waited, watching her smile stay and stay, until she put her hands on the table and brought her face to mine.

"Let's do it," she said.

I ran to the man with golden teeth and hollered for our check. "Snap, snap, Mr Wonderful," I said. "*We* are getting married!"

"I no tell you a lie, eh? We take care of you."

"You're beautiful, my friend," I said, and meant it.

And then Robin appeared. "What's the matter," she said, "are the alien's coming?"

"We, Robin, are getting married."

"Well, can you feature that?"

I grabbed her face and gave it a giant kiss. "You are a freaking angel."

Robin waggled her silver ball. "The more you give, the better it is," she said. "Empty your cup!"

From the phone booth outside we called a cab, and the next thing we knew, we were at the County Clerk's applying for a license to get hitched. Avey and I both were as amazed by how well the world seemed to work, given the mayhem it had been cast into, as we had been by the mayhem at its peak. Last night, we were trapped in a cabin on a mountain that snatched up the life of our friend and set us fearing for our own. Today, our friend was gone, and we were eating crepes and eggs in a diner full of merrymaking fools, and rushing off to marriage. You never know what's coming for you, I said to Avey. And what's coming for you, Avey said, is always what's best, even if you don't know it. That was good enough for me, then: she was holding my hand. I told the preacher who answered the number off our list we needed someone to make quick work of two desperate lovers.

"Chomping at the old bit are you?" the reverend said as though he were hard of hearing.

"Right now," I said. "Can you do it?"

"Think you can hold the old horses for about an hour?"

"What time is it?" I said.

"Noon, of course," he said. "Listen. The old wife's got left-over turkey and stuffing on the table as we speak."

"Where're you located?"

"I'll tell you what, son. We aren't going anywheres today, what with this infernal weather. If you can be here by one, we'll be pleased as punch to do you right."

Good thing we'd hit the Wells Fargo inside Raley's before heading to the diner. I'd left just two bucks in my account, the balance a fire in my pocket. To hell with Super, to hell with Basil and Lucille. We didn't need them. The cab would cost plenty, that much we knew, but I didn't care and neither did my girl.

Our driver was a tiny guy, smaller than me, a hundred pounds, if that. He looked a lot like the rat from *Reservoir Dogs*, actually, the one with the scrawny van dyke and yellowy teeth played by Steve Buscemi, an impression that sealed when he crammed a thumb against a nostril and honked some junk from the other. A scarcely concealed agitation entered his voice when we told him our destination.

"Lucky for you it's slow today," he said. "I don't normally go nowhere past Elk Point."

No doubt his attitude changed after I said there'd be an extra twenty in the deal if he'd shut his mouth and drive. For about fifteen minutes everything was peachy, me and my mud-paddy necking away like a couple of teenaged horn dogs. But there's always something, and the car began to shudder.

"What the hell?" I said.

"Didn't nobody tell me the gas gauge was busted."

"Look," I said. "We're on our way to get married."

"So what do you want, a toaster?"

"Maybe you could get on the horn," Avey said, "and call somebody. Think you can do that?"

The twerp picked up his radio and turned a couple of knobs. "For your sake I'll pretend I didn't hear nothing." He rolled down the window and waved his hand at the world. "I don't hear nothing but the cars passing by."

When we pulled up at the reverend's nearly an hour on, an old man and woman were in their garage, between two cars.

"Are you Reverend Rumsey?" I said.

A short man with a handlebar mustache and thinning hair, he wore a black wool blazer and collarless shirt played up by a diamond in gold, the size of a Canadian dime. "Friends call me Rev-Up," he said, and noted the plates on his car. REV UP, it said, opposite the other, JMP 4 JOY. "Just like that," the man said, "only with a hyphen."

"You were going to conduct a service for us."

"You know what time it is, son?"

"We had a blowout on the way up." I gestured toward the ratman. "Our cab."

"One-thirty," said Rev-Up. "Or thereabouts."

Avey flashed her best sad frown. "You said you weren't going out today."

"I said I wasn't going out for *work*. Me and the old gal got thirsty."

"So you're not going to marry us."

"Did I say that?" Rev-Up stepped to the door of the car his wife had got in and said, "Looks like they're here, Dale."

The place was warm and bright and smelled of potpourri and burning wood and mincemeat pie and spuds.

"Now I'm not criticizing you," Rev-Up said, "but why in the heck did you kids choose today of all days to tie the old knot?"

Avey slapped her legs. "It's another one of those real-long-stories deals," she said.

"We know all about *those*," said Dale. Her rhinestone brooch, in the shape of a cross, twinkled in the lights from the Xmas tree. "If only we had a nickel for every time we've heard that line—"

"—we'd be gazillionaires," said Rev-Up. He was twisting the tips of his stache. Funny I hadn't noticed, but his fingers were those of a woman, long and slender and tapered at the ends, with longish nails, too, that looked like they'd been shellacked. He was the type of guy, I saw, who studied his stamps in panties he nabbed from his wife. He finished with his twiddling and took a pipe from beside a red glass bowl of candy. "Any particular angle," he asked, "you want to the service?"

"I've never gone in for too much Bible pounding," I said. "No offense."

"None taken," Rev-Up said. He drew at his pipe and twiddled his stache. "Hows about some good old-fashioned spirituals then?"

"What do you think?" I said to Avey.

"With them," said Rev-Up, "it's about the Great Spirit and such-like."

All this talk was making me nervous. It didn't matter to me what the man said, so long as it was legal.

"Personally," Rev-Up said, "for my money, I'd go with old Heyzoose Himself. The New Testament, straight down the line. But that's just me, of course."

"The other stuff sounded good to me," said Avey.

Rev-Up looked to see I was with her. "Then the other stuff it shall be. Any time you two're ready."

Avey didn't have a veil. Dale offered a rhinestone tiara, but Avey took my snowcap, the one I'd got from Dinky, and garnished it with toilet paper, green. And there we were, hand-in-hand to Rev-Up's voice, sonorous and warm. "It is," I heard him say, "an important moment when two people, who at one time were strangers to one another, are drawn together by an irresistible force, so that, henceforth, their lives will not be divided by space or by time..." And later a bit of Kahlil Gibran snuck into the picture, something about singing and dancing in the midst of being alone. "The strings of a lute," Rev-Up intoned, "though they quiver with the same music, are alone. And you will stand together, yet not too near together, for the pillars of the temple stand apart, and the oak and the cypress grow not in each other's shadow... You are performing an act of complete and utter faith..." And then my head went south, a misty curtain draping from the wings. Rev-Up was asking for the symbols of our commitment. It took a minute to find the rings we'd got from the gumball machine at the diner. Our man was dismayed when he saw them, but discretely forged ahead. "These rings are a symbol in this your wedding ceremony and in your marriage of two things. First, they are made of a material that does not tarnish, and this symbolizes your love for one another remaining forever pure and untarnished. Second, they are made in a complete circle, having no beginning and no end. This, too, symbolizes your love for one another, remaining forever."

A minute later found me saying, "With this ring I thee wed. Let it ever be to us a symbol of our eternal love," and a minute later yet Rev-Up said, "By the authority vested in me by my church and by the state of Nevada, I now pronounce you husband and wife. You may kiss each other!"

And then Avey was on my back. Snow had somehow appeared, or maybe it had been there always, I don't know, but we were piggybacking through the stuff, and falling in the stuff, and laughing and kissing and laughing. Just across the way an old pair of Czechs had set up a store that sold us cheap champagne. The ratman told us we were nuts, and we laughingly agreed.

BACK AT THE MOTEL, WE FOUND SUPER IN HIS truck with his Pall Mall, Fortinbras as ever by his side.

"We have the curious suspicion something heterodoxical's in the air."

"Super," I said, "meet Avey vanden Heuvel, my new wife."

"Well, well," Super said. "Isn't that a thrifty board you've set."

"I don't catch your drift."

"What's to catch? There's not a fool this side of the pass that can't see the funeral-baked meats'll do fine for the marital feast. If that's not thrift, we don't know it." The old man clapped me on the shoulder and said his heart was glad. Then, with a stiff but passionate dip of his head, he took Avey's hand and kissed it. "Reap while you can, butterfly," he said. "Reap while you can."

In our room, alone at last, we dallied in love till solitude took us, followed by dreamless sleep. We woke to the sounds of laughter. The room now was black, I didn't know where I was. Something brushed my cheek, a strand of hair, I thought, that made me think of a man I'd known, who when he saw hair on a motel bed thought it from a Turk. It's true how rooms like these harbor what's left of others, bits of tawdry fact crying out from time—the illegible guest books and marked-up scriptures in the Gideons by the bed, a forgotten pair of panties beneath the mattress and burns on the stand, the solitary clip of nail that scrapes your feet and conjures to mind this day or that long past. Once, as a child, my family had stayed at the only motel in town. Death Valley was the place, or maybe some dump near the waste that is Needles. It was hot and dry and dark, with a skyful of stars I remember as sad. The clerk that night had stepped out for a smoke and seen me by the fence round the pool, staring at the water. *Don't go getting any far out ideas*, he'd said, *about sticking your tootsies in that, my friend. But it's so hot*, I said. *You don't figure that fence ain't there for nothing, do you?* he said. I asked what he meant, and he knelt in the rocks and told of the boy who'd drowned last year, a boy, in fact, about my age. His parents had put him to bed and gone to eat, then come back to a TV lost in fuzz. It wasn't till morning, after they'd phoned the police and firemen and county sheriff too that the man himself found the kid, floating in the pool by a little dead mouse. All my life I'd remember that story. And more than once I'd find myself thinking of the lights in the pool, the boy above, luminescent, void, bobbing with the ripples of the cruising snake…

Avey stirred at my side, I rose to the surface, I knew where I was, on solid ground at last.

"Open up, you fools," Basil shouted.

I went to the door in a blanket. Lucille had a cocktail, a bourbon and coke on a pile of ice, and was smiling like a little girl.

"What have we here?" Basil said.

"Some hanky panky no doubt," Lucille said.

"We got married," Avey said.

"That's just about the most stupidest thing I ever heard," Basil said.

"This calls for a celebration!" Lucille said.

"We don't want a celebration," Avey said, and hid beneath the sheets.

"But it's New Year's Eve," Basil said.

"And it's still my party," Lucille said. "Besides, that's what Dinky would've wanted."

Basil flipped the lights. "*Get on uppa!*" he sang, doing his best James Brown.

"Basil won 600 bucks at the table," Lucille said.

"What about the Cruiser?" Avey said.

"It's totaled," Lucille said.

"We'll rent a car tomorrow," Basil said.

"We're going to tear this place up," Lucille said, and emptied a bag on the bureau, bourbon and cokes and magazines and smokes and beer. "It took us a while to get things right," she said, "but now we're back on track." She spun round to Basil. "Turn on some music, squeeze."

"Ah baby, for Pete's sake, when're you going to stop that?"

"Squeeze got a boom box," Lucille said.

"Magnavox," Basil said. "A hundred and sixty-nine bones at K-Mart." He flipped a switch and out came "Let Me Drown." "So you really did it?" he said. Avey held up her hand. "What's that?"

"My wedding ring of course."

"You got a problem with it?" I said.

"It's from a box of Cracker Jacks."

"Gumball machine," I said. "Twenty-five cents."

"When are you going to pop the question to me, honey-buns?" said Lucille.

"See what you went and did?" Basil said.

"You know Chris Rock," Avey said.

"Do I know Chris Rock," Basil said. "Of course I know Chris Rock. I know everything."

"Then you've heard his routine about the old man in the club."

"I haven't," Lucille said.

"'You don't get married,' he says, 'pretty soon you'll find yourself a single man, too old for the club. Not really old, just a little bit too old to be in the club.'"

"He's already too old to be in the club," I said.

"Fix yourself a drink," Basil said. "For some crazy reason, I'm in a decent mood."

We took turns in the shower, slamming cocktails as we went. None of what had happened had happened at all, it seemed. No one mentioned Dinky. Everyone was happy. It was like we were truly friends.

As for the rest of the world, it too may as well have forgotten the storm with all its havoc. Up on the strip, from state line to Caesar's, the 50 was jammed with boobs galore.

Oily women with giant hair and turquoise jewels squealed at their men. His hand trembling with uncertainty or hope, a one-legged man spooned sugar on a napkin. When a cocktail girl with tits so big they had to've cost ten grand apiece asked the man his pleasure, he stuck a fifty in her cleavage and said, "Hows about twenty with you?" Blackjack dealers dealt their cards and waited for deliverance. A bald man flung his toupee at a man with too much hair while a tubby guy in spandex on a circular stage crooned "Tiny Bubbles" so well Don Ho would've liked to see him dead. Everywhere we went, obscenity and artifice swam in the general eye. Voices sang out, grunts were heard, the smell of money and booze and costly steaks oozed from every door.

Basil paid a bag lady dripping with mud five crazy dollars for a photo of our bunch. Super appeared and disappeared, we could never say why or how. A woman at least three hundred pounds hit the jackpot on a dollar machine, then burst into a fit of laughter. When her money spilled from the pan, she dropped to the floor and rolled among the coins. The night raged on. Hostesses in corsets handed drinks to any who asked, the world was overjoyed. I clung to Avey and she to me, we were hugging and kissing and laughing and shouting and tripping and stumbling and shouting. And then we heard a drunk cry out midnight was on its way.

We found ourselves in the street, on the state line outside Harrah's. All around people had joined hands and begun to rally in a single line, twisting and turning as the countdown neared. I tried to keep up but tripped in the gutter, a strange hand before me, and five behind it. I hadn't yet reached my feet when, dimly at first, a voice rolled through the crowd. Only after it had swelled to a roar did I know it was the voice of the crowd itself, a unified chant, counting down from ten.

I stood up. Faces had turned to the sky. When the roar descended to the number zero, rockets went sighing to the heavens and exploded all around. That was it, then, midnight, no longer New Year's Eve, not yet New Year's Day. Everyone was kissing everyone, you couldn't have stopped them if you tried. A thousand laughing faces, every single face, had melded into one. We spun in circles, Avey and I, round and round, until the dizziness took us, and we fell into the crowd. Goddamn, it was a celebration.

## Gratitude

I have so many people in my life who've done so much for me in so many ways, I hardly know where to begin to thank you all. If you're not here, but know you should be, I hope you won't be too hard: it's my oversight entirely.

Jeanine, Jeanine, Jeanine, without whom this book wouldn't be.

Bharati, who supported me when I didn't deserve support and gave me the best advice a writer could have, what kept me going all those times I wanted to stop: I've never forgotten, Bharati, I am so grateful.

Clark, man of wisdom and grace.

Hillary, who knows why.

Tony, through thick and thin.

Andy, who's always had my back.

James, absurd hustler, artiste supreme, bad motherfucker, my man.

Eric, who saw what no one else had seen, then walked his talk the way we've all come to appreciate (and expect).

Eliza, powerhouse extraordinaire.

And, in no special order, for reasons big and small (you all know why, too):

Augustus Rose, Nami Mun, Jennifer Deitz, Nick Petrulakis, Bridget Hoida, Jenn Stroud Rossman, John Beckman, Snorri Sturluson, Sean Madigan Hoen, Neil Wiltshire, Brendan Burke, Stephen Stralka, Jack Hicks, Brett Beutel, Butch O'Brien, TT O'Brien, Janis Finwall, Todd O'Brien, Christopher O'Brien, Tim O'Brien, Mary DeMartinis, Lauren O'Brien, Christian Kiefer, Xander Cameron, David Gutowski, Gabrielle Gantz, Jason Diamond, Karolina Waclawiak, Jeff Jackson, Joshua Mohr, Anne-Marie Kinney, Grace Krilanovich,

Barbara Browning, Don DeLillo, Emily Gould, Matthew Specktor, Gabino Iglesias, Luke Goebel, Richard Nash, Terese Svoboda, Adam Wilson, Jocelyn Tobias, Samuel Sattin, Mike Young, Cari Luna, Robbie Egan, Mark Cugini, Gregory Henry, Adam Robinson, Benjamin Dreyer, Scott McClanahan, Laura van den Berg, Halimah Marcus, Deborah Hay, Hilary Clark, Eric Palmerlee, Andrea Johnston, Molly Poerstel, Ros Warby, Sher Doriff, Luke Degnan, Oona Patrick, Stephen Corey, Mindy Wilson, Germán Sierra, Cal Morgan, Kyle Minor, Stephen Dunn, Brian Bouldrey, Nicole Elizabeth, Lauren Cerand, Molly Gaudry, Renee Zuckerbrot, Chris Parris-Lamb, Andrea Coates, Michael J Seidlinger, Oren Moverman, Brian Bennett, Victor Giganti, Eddie Evanisko, Michele Durning, Douglas Durning, Carole Doughty, Joseph Fuqua, Ben Austin, Anneke Hansen, Daniel Scott, David Duhr, Deborah Lohse, Eddy Rathke, Erika Anderson, Penina Roth, Graham Storey, Major West, Leslie O'Neill, Gregg Holtgrewe, Julian Barnett, Daniel Sullivan, Julie Mayo, Melissa Maino, Ron Tanner, Ryan Johnston, Jason Ross, Sean H. Doyle, Susie DeFord, Tamara Ober, Virginia Konchan, Will Jones, Michael Harris, Scott Cheshire, Alice Peck, Jason Russo, Virginia Hatt, Kashana Cauley, Christine Onorati, Emily Pullen, Jenn Northington, Mark Snyder, WORD Books, Monica Westin, Aaron Garson, Caitlin Elizabeth Harper, Elvis Alves, Donald Ray Pollock, Joseph Salvatore, Jean-Pierre Karwacki, Deb Cameron, Adam Pieroni, Jennifer Pieroni, Minna Proctor, Renée Ashley, David Daniel, Jeff Johnson, Jen Loy, Kaya Oakes, Jennifer McCulloch, Kymba Bartley, Boris Hauf, Litó Walkey, Martin Nachbar, Zoë Knights, Austin Wilson, Brooks Sterritt, Julia Fierro…

Also published by **TWO DOLLAR RADIO**

## MIRA CORPORA
A NOVEL BY JEFF JACKSON

"This novel is like nothing I've ever read before and is, unquestionably, one of my favorite books published this year."
—Laura van den Berg, *Salon*

"A piercing howl of a book. This punk coming-of-age story smolders long after the book is through." —*Slate*

## NOTHING
A NOVEL BY ANNE MARIE WIRTH CAUCHON

"Apocalyptic and psychologically attentive. I was moved."
—Tao Lin, *New York Times Book Review*

"A riveting first piece of scripture from our newest prophet of misspent youth." —*Paste*

"The energy almost makes each page glow. Though this novel starts as Bret Easton Ellis, it ends as Nick Cave – thunderous, apocalyptic." —*Electric Literature's 'The Outlet'*

## THE ORANGE EATS CREEPS
A NOVEL BY GRACE KRILANOVICH

- National Book Foundation 2010 '5 Under 35' Selection.
- *NPR* Best Books of 2010.
- *The Believer* Book Award Finalist.

"Krilanovich's work will make you believe that new ways of storytelling are still emerging from the margins." —*NPR*

## A QUESTIONABLE SHAPE
A NOVEL BY BENNETT SIMS

"[*A Questionable Shape*] is more than just a novel. It is literature. It is life."
—*The Millions*

"Presents the yang to the yin of Whitehead's *Zone One*, with chess games, a dinner invitation, and even a romantic excursion. Echoes of [Thomas] Bernhard's hammering circularity and [David Foster] Wallace's bright min that can't stop making connections are both present. The point is where the mind goes, and, in that respect, Sims has his thematic territory down cold." —*The Daily Beast*